Stolen Recipes AND A Dead Chef

MJ MILLER

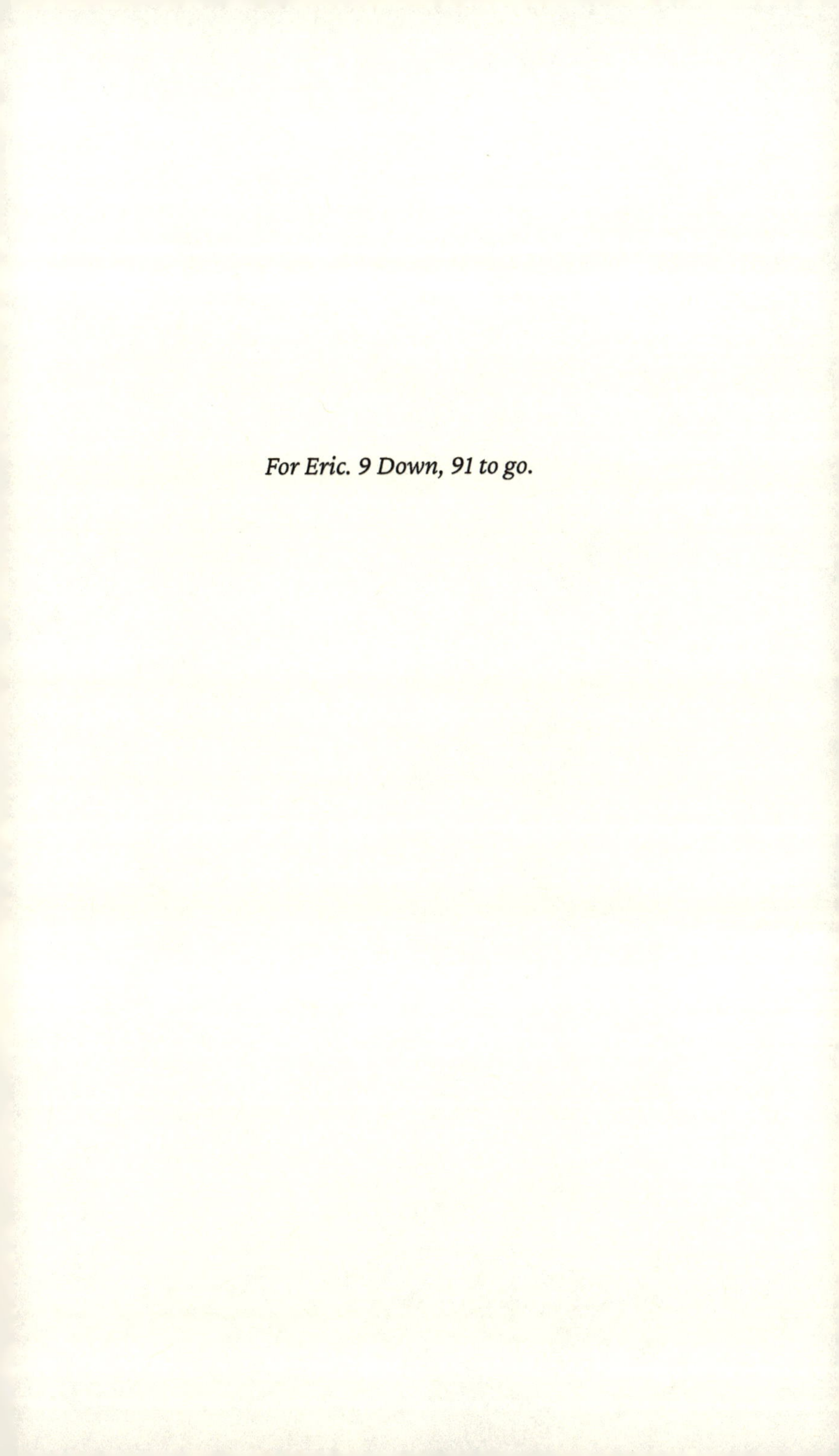

For Eric. 9 Down, 91 to go.

TRADEMARK ACKNOWLEDGEMENTS

- Kemosabe The Lone Ranger: NBC Universal
- *Helen Reddy*
- Ziegfeld Follies Public Domain
- *Barbara Streisand*
- OuijaHasbro Inc
- Sherlock *Conan Doyle Estate Ltd*
- Pinterest Pintrest Inc
- YouTubeGoogle, inc, subsidiary of Alphabet, Inc
- Hot Lips Walt Disney Co.
- Curious George Houghton Mifflin Company
- Sylvester the Cat Warner Brothers
- Addams Family Paramount Pictures
- It's a Wonderful Life NBC Universal
- TikTok Byte Dance
- *Madonna*
- Christmas Vacation PalmStar Media
- Watson *Conan Doyle Estate Ltd*
- *The Raskins,*
- Lolita—1955 novel written by Vladimir Nabokov
- *Lucille Ball*
- *Doris Day*
- *Meyer Davis*
- 48 Hours (TV show CBS)
- Poise Kimberly Clark
- *Marvin Gaye*
- *Dolly Parton*

- The Rockettes MSG Entertainment
- *Fanny Brice*
- Jell-O (Kraft Heinz)
- Ghostbusters Columbia Pictures
- All I want for Christmas Mariah Carey & Walter Afanasieff (writers and producers)
- Alvin, Simon, and Theodore (Alvin and the Chipmunks Bagdasarian Productions)
- Rockin' Around the Christmas Tree (song written by Johnny Marks and recorded by Brenda Lee in 1958)
- *Jon Bon Jovi*
- Golden Girls (TV show) Disney Enterprises
- Sophia (from Golden Girls) Disney Enterprises
- *Springsteen*
- *Rod Stewart.*
- Yelp Yelp
- Hummer General Motors
- Jeep Fiat/Chrysler
- iPad Apple Inc
- ClueHasbro
- Dirty Dancing Vestron Pictures
- James Beard Foundation Award
- EpiPen Myland
- Holiday Inn IHG

CHAPTER ONE

I glanced at the text, then at Billy, one of the pigmy goats we'd recently adopted, but before I could react, Devon sprinted into the yard, a look of horror on his face.

Devon Marks did not wear horror well. He was a finely honed, smoking-hot chief of police who happened to be my brave, never frightened by much, significant other.

"What happened?" My heart banged the inside of my ribs, and a tic in my right eye twitched. This year, as the proud new homeowners of Luckland's finest reno project, we were doing the honors of hosting Thanksgiving dinner, and the thought of something going wrong had my adrenaline pumping.

Instead of answering, he pointed to the house. Fearing someone had gotten hurt, I raced through the back door to find my mom and her besties, the infamous Luckland Ladies, or as I affectionally called them, the posse, standing in a circle and staring down at something, or someone, on the floor. My mother, Kate, fluttered like a fairy. Matilda, Devon's mom, stood calmly next to her. Prudence tried not to laugh while

Hope and Marcy, the only two who belonged in the kitchen, wore curious frowns.

If there was going to be a calamity on Thanksgiving, I should have known they would be involved—though they didn't usually start tipping the bottle till at least noon. Since my twin sister Babs hadn't yet arrived, who or what lay on the floor was anyone's guess.

Finally noticing me, they broke the circle and allowed me to peer in.

"Who did this?" I looked closely at each of the women. All five turned toward Devon, who stood in the doorway. I focused my attention on him.

"Devon, my culinary wonder, is this your doing?" I pointed to the floor where sat the unfortunate victim.

"I'm afraid so, Pip," he said as a blush crept into his cheeks.

"How?"

"I don't know. It was like someone had greased him up. I couldn't keep hold of him." He shook his head, quite contrite with his puppy dog face. I melted.

"It's okay. I had a premonition the other day something like this would happen. So, I bought a spare. It's in the fridge in the garage."

I, Pippa O'Leary, was nothing if not prepared. I'd had a hunch several days earlier that something would happen to our Thanksgiving bird, though I couldn't determine what. Devon was a wonder in the kitchen. Tom Turkey going splat on my kitchen floor was...strange. Maybe supernaturally strange. Or ladies strange.

While Devon hurried off to fetch the turkey's replacement, I acknowledged that trying to host Thanksgiving in a home still going through renovations was monstrously over-ambitious. We'd only just finished our kitchen remodel. Admitting defeat, I let out a shrill whistle to stop the women's chatter.

"Change of plans. I think we should prepare our feast elsewhere. There's some bad mojo in here." I looked at the women, knowing they'd agree.

Bad mojo was what they called the mystical happenings we'd recently all experienced in and around Luckland, specifically in my house we'd named Mystic Manor. With otherworldly apparitions, odd noises, and spooky sightings, Luckland was living up to its legend. Well, at least one of them.

Matilda nodded. "Right you are, Pip. Ladies? Let's take this over to the Inn, shall we?" They set to work gathering up the bags and baskets of food they'd brought and hustled out our front door.

When Devon returned with the backup bird, I told him about the change in plans.

He sighed. "Sorry, Red, I know you really wanted to host Thanksgiving."

I smiled at what I now considered an endearment. Growing up, when he called me Red, I usually looked for the nearest projectile to toss his way. "Only because *you* wanted to. You haven't had Thanksgiving with the posse in over ten years."

Devon's recent return home was just the start of a whole lot of changes in our cozy little town, and our personal lives.

"I'm sure it hasn't changed, and you know why I couldn't attend celebration dinners. FBI remember? Crime doesn't take a holiday."

"You remember it that well?" I circled him, gently poking him every so often to make a point. "Who's bringing sweet potatoes?"

"Prudence. Spiked with a fifth of rum." He grinned, exposing the dimple on his right cheek.

"Green bean casserole?" I asked.

"Your mom. Always. She claims it's the easiest."

"Crescent rolls?"

"Mom, who will also make the creamed corn." He raised an eyebrow.

"Oh no, Dev, we don't bother with that anymore."

Devon's smile fell. "She always makes creamed corn."

"Well, the thing is, since you never made it home for the holidays, she quit making it."

Maybe I'd gone too far in teasing the poor man. He did love his creamed corn. I leaned up and kissed his wonderfully handsome face. "Don't worry, I know for a fact there'll be your fave on the table. So, what shall we bring? Aside from a turkey."

"A case of wine? Because there's no way in hell we'll survive without it." He grinned, gave me a wink, and put his arms around me. It was perfect timing for my phone to buzz.

"Incoming text?" he asked, curious.

I glanced at my phone, then sighed. "From Babs."

Emergency. Luckland Inn.

CHAPTER TWO

There were a thousand or more things I might have envisioned Babs could have meant when she texted there was an emergency. However, when we pulled up in front of the Luckland Inn, the disaster that played out on the sidewalk was beyond anything I could have dreamed.

My fraternal twin sister was always put together. Neat as a pin with never a hair out of place. She could have been the poster girl for the perfect holiday hostess in her trim, white winter jumpsuit. However, with green goo oozing down her body, she now resembled the poster girl for Ghostbusters. I wasn't sure how to react. My devilish side craved a big grin, while my sisterhood side wanted to reach out and hug her.

Before I stepped out of the car, Devon put his hand on my arm.

"Easy, Red. We have no idea how this happened. No sense riling her up."

"Understood, Kemosabe, but if you'd had siblings, you'd understand the sacrifice I'm about to make."

One side of his mouth pulled up as he shook his head.

As I approached Babs, I stifled my snicker and put on my

sisterly face, all concern and empathy, though I wished to god I'd brought my camera so I could capture the moment of Babs O'Leary-Cornwall covered in...whatever that was. Normally, bad things happened to me, so it was a nice change not to be on the receiving end.

Just then, my mother came running out the door, towels in hand, muttering something about a Sylvester.

I glanced at Devon, who seemed just as bewildered as me. We turned as my mother began wiping the goo, which looked like Jell-O, off Babs. Mom's efforts didn't work very well as Babs's lovely white jumpsuit took on a distinctly lime-colored hue. The more Mom rubbed, the greener the jumpsuit got. All we needed were some cinnamon candies to sprinkle on Babs, and we'd have had a winter wonderland cupcake in front of us. It didn't help that my mom, all five feet two inches of her, wore some sort of harvest holiday apron and an orange jumpsuit eerily similar to my sister's. I suspected they'd gone shopping together, as they often did. Mom's blonde hair, neatly trimmed in a bob, peeked out from beneath a pinecone hat. Considering my mom had just left Mystic Manor a few minutes earlier, her clothing baffled me. I knew for sure she'd worn jeans and a sweatshirt in my kitchen when she tsked over the turkey because my mom in a sweatshirt was an event not to be over-looked or forgotten.

"Devon, I have a horrible suspicion the posse somehow knew they'd end up here." I kept my voice low, though I was sure neither my sister nor my mother paid any attention to us.

"Hmm" Devon pursed his lips, then began biting the inside of his cheek. A sure sign of contemplation. "Do you think they greased the turkey?"

"I don't know, but I wouldn't put it past them."

"Wouldn't put what past whom?" my mom asked.

I grinned. "Nothing. So, what happened to you, Babs?"

"Sylvester," she said as she gently cleansed her face with a washcloth my mom handed to her.

"Who is Sylvester?" Devon whispered to me.

"No clue," I whispered back. "Let's find out." I took his hand and pulled him along to the main door of the Luckland Inn—where we were stopped short by a furry. AKA a human in animal costume. Sylvester the Cat. One mystery solved.

Sylvester wasn't the only surprise. A large group milled about the lobby of the Inn—squirrels, rabbits, and a fox mingled together in perfect harmony. I'd heard about furries, but this was the first time I'd been up close and personal with them, and I wondered what they were doing here because the Inn was technically closed for renovation.

Hope and Marcy, owners of the Blue Sky Café, had recently purchased the Inn along with the attached bakery. They'd already moved the café to the bakery but were still working on a few updates to the Inn.

The previous owners had remodeled and modernized the rooms upstairs, so they no longer resembled a brothel—the Inn's original purpose when built sometime in the late eighteen hundreds, but the lobby was eerily authentic. The original floor needed a good sanding and staining, and the chandelier wouldn't have looked out of place in a haunted house, which the Inn was purported to be. There had been many rumored sightings over the years of the Scarlet Lady. I never quite figured out whether scarlet referred to the dress she wore or perhaps something more gruesome.

"Devon, Devon, over here!" Trey, Devon's biological dad, who'd gone MIA for thirty years or so but had recently rekindled his relationship with Devon's mom, called from the front desk. Devon headed over. He leaned on the desk and listened while Trey waved his arms and pointed here and there as he spoke. Devon nodded, then indicated I should approach.

I leaned up against the desk and mimicked Devon's posture. "So, what's happening in here? Other than green goo disasters and a woodland creature's conference?"

"Oh, Pippa, I'm afraid this is all my fault. Tillie asked me to mind the desk last week while she ran off with the girls somewhere. The phone rang. I answered it just as she instructed. You know, 'Luckland Inn, can I help you?'" Trey shook his head and swallowed hard. "The woman on the phone, at least I think she was a woman, said they needed rooms to ring in the holidays. I assumed that meant Christmas or New Year's."

"Of course, Trey, anyone would," Devon said to reassure him.

"When she said the twenty-fifth, I assumed she meant December. You know, Christmas. Turns out, she meant Thanksgiving."

Understanding dawned on me. "They've booked a few days, and now they're here."

"Yes, yes, and so we have no choice. I guess we have extra guests for dinner. And only one turkey."

"Aren't they vegan?" I turned to look at the impromptu guests. "Why don't we add some vegetable and pasta casseroles."

Trey shook his head. "No, not vegan at all. In fact, when they got here, and I realized I'd misunderstood, they made it clear they were looking forward to a real feast. These folks don't have anywhere to celebrate, it seems, so they all get together with one another."

"You seem to know a lot about furries, Trey," Devon said, his tone curious.

"I've run into them now and again on the road. They're much like Trekkies and those who dress up at comic-cons. Same thing. Just a bit of cosplay."

I found that interesting. I'd never put much thought into furry culture. Perhaps I needed to read up on them.

———

After Babs's slime fiasco, which had happened when Sylvester had accidentally knocked into her while she navigated the group of furries with her notorious green gelatin salad held high above her head, she'd gone home and changed. I saw her enter the lobby about an hour later with my brother-in-law Tom and my niece Leah, who wore antlers in honor of the unexpected guests. As requested by me, Babs had also brought in my spare camera from the ladies' huge RV parked in Prudence's driveway. As an outdoor photographer, I wasn't often caught ill-equipped, so I thanked her and promised to take photos of Leah as a memento of the celebration.

We set up the private party room for the furries, as the rest of us would be dining at the big wooden table in the formal dining room. As *luck* would have it, Hope and Marcy had several turkeys available—confirming my suspicion they'd planned to host Thanksgiving all along. The ladies were just humoring Devon and me when we offered to host the big feast. I didn't know how, but without a doubt, they'd buttered up that turkey when Devon was otherwise occupied. I made a mental note to ask about those *spare turkeys.*

I truly hoped the rest of the day would go off without a hitch. However, this was Luckland, where nothing was ever as it seemed, so there was a strong probability that "Turkey Day" would become one more of Luckland's legendary tall tales waiting to be told and retold every year.

After taking several photos of the furry crowd and my gorgeous three-year-old niece, I tucked my camera safely in the office, then offered to help in the kitchen.

"What can I do to help?" I asked Marcy, who seemed to be in charge.

"Chestnuts. For the stuffing. Just cook those up in the microwave, then peel and cut in quarters if you would."

I may not have been a culinary goddess, but I could manage simple tasks. I placed the chestnuts on a plate and put them in the microwave. While I waited for them to cook, I began to gather what I'd need to prepare them. Popping commenced, and I assumed the chestnuts must cook like popcorn. That would make them easy to peel.

"Pippa, you did score them, didn't you?" Marcy's voice came across higher pitched than usual.

"Score?"

"Oh my god! You didn't..."

I didn't know I was supposed to score the shells with an X so they didn't explode. The cacophony of chestnuts detonating inside the microwave brought a crowd of furries into the kitchen to see what was happening.

Marcy quickly shooed me out of the kitchen even though I offered to clean up the mess. Apparently, I was now persona non grata.

"Here, Pip, you do this," Hope said as she shoved a cardboard box in my hands. It was a big box, especially for tiny little Hope. She wore one of her signature pencil skirt and blazer outfits in a muted orange in honor of the holidays. Her hair, which she styled every morning, she'd arranged in one of her updos.

Inside the box were snow globes and what appeared to be a full set of *It's a Wonderful Life* holiday town figurines.

"Me?"

"Of course, we're going to need photos to promote the holidays here at the Inn."

"And you want me to decorate?"

"Don't be silly. We want you to photograph everything. You're the one with the creative eye. You'll know what will work in the photos, so you might as well put the holiday decor out where it works best."

That was basically her way of asking me to decorate and take photos without *asking*. Clever trick. I sighed and set the box down behind me at the desk.

"Anything else?" I muttered somewhat sarcastically toward her retreating form as she scurried away.

As I started unpacking the box, Finn, the newly anointed Inn manager after faithfully serving the Blue Sky Café for several years between archaeology expeditions, ran up to me, breathing heavily.

"Finn? What's up?"

He shook his phone in front of my face. I quickly grabbed the phone before I got banged on the nose with it.

A TikTok video. He was a big fan. Me, not so much. I humored him and played it. The footage showed a flashing neon holiday sign that read "The only good furry is a dead one" over blurry footage of a furry, possibly a polar bear, lying on its side in an alley. The problem, aside from the horrid message, was the alley in the video looked to be the one behind the Inn, as signified by the dumpster in the background—the one that said Blue Sky Café on it.

I grabbed my phone and fired off a text to Devon.

Me: Emergency. Alley. Dead polar bear.

CHAPTER THREE

FINN AND I RACED OUT BACK, ARRIVING TO FIND DEVON SHINING HIS flashlight in wide circles. Though not yet five o'clock, it was already dark, the late November sun setting earlier and earlier.

"Polar bears?" he asked, one eyebrow raised. Clearly there was nothing in the alley. Not even the Blue Sky dumpster.

"Finn," I demanded. "Show him."

Finn handed his phone to Devon with the video queued up.

Devon watched the video a few times, then handed the phone back to Finn.

"Maybe just a practical joke," Devon said, then he narrowed his eyes and strode toward the end of the building where a black wrought iron gate blocked traffic. He shone his light on a white polar bear costume draped over the wrought iron spears. The costume had a large, round, red stain in the middle. Finn and I leaned forward. Neither of us wanted to get any closer, we just wanted to see.

"Back up, you two," Devon said quietly as he pulled his police radio out of his pocket. He called for backup, and not long after, sirens blared in the distance.

Deputy Martin, Prudence's beau, came barreling around the

corner. Barely pausing to acknowledge us, he shouted for us to get inside. We did, taking our place right inside the doorway where we could poke out our heads—until he pushed the door closed.

"Well, that was something." Devon shook his head as he and Martin came back in a few minutes later.

"What? What was something?" Finn demanded. I darted him a look, warning him to let Devon talk.

"Come on, Inspector, give it up. What was it?" I wasn't known for my patience either.

"Cranberry sauce," Martin said. "Pretty sure."

"Wait, what?" I knew what he meant but didn't quite believe him.

"Cranberry sauce. Not blood. And considering how wet the costume was, I think someone just hung it there to dry."

"And the video?" Finn asked. "Someone in that costume was lying on the ground."

"I'm gonna guess by the smell they had a little too much good cheer and heaved it." Martin smirked and shared an uninterpretable glance with Devon. I figured they were making a silent comment on the polar bear's inability to hold his liquor.

Certainly not a pleasant thought. I appreciated the good news that there was no homicidal maniac in a bunny suit murdering guests—however, the best part of Thanksgiving for me was crashing on the couch, stuffed as a goose, and watching Christmas Vacation. Instead, I was stuck at the Luckland Inn with furries and chaos.

Devon snuck up behind me and nuzzled my neck. I looked up and grinned at the mistletoe in his hand.

After that, Thanksgiving dinner seemed to go smoothly. I

helped clear dishes and coordinated the serving of the pies—an annual tradition whereby everyone helped themselves to a gluttonous and inappropriate number of pies. Then Devon and I took a breath and grabbed a furtive kiss or two in the lobby.

"Whaddya say, ginger snap? Should we sneak out?" Devon whispered in my ear.

I grinned and grabbed his hand. "Quick, while we can," I whispered back as I tugged him toward the door. We probably could have made a quick getaway had we not paused under the mistletoe.

"Yoo-hoo! Devon, my boy! Pippa!" Matilda's sing-song voice made me almost groan as she came up right behind us.

We turned. "Mom, yes, what is it?" Devon asked, his expression patient.

"We've got just a teensy-weensy problem."

In Luckland, there was no such thing as a teensy-weensy problem. Only major fiascos around every corner.

"What might that be?" I asked, keeping my tone neutral.

"Well, you know we like to keep the guests entertained, so we set up some karaoke for them. But they're not cooperating at all. I'm afraid there's a brawl brewing."

Devon sighed and raised his brows. "A brawl?"

"Seems Alvin, Simon, and Theodore have chosen *All I Want for Christmas,* and Sylvester is quite upset about it."

"And why would that be?" I asked.

"Because they changed the words." Matilda pursed her lips, holding in a smirk. "Seems they want two buxom blondes, and Sylvester, it turns out, is a priest."

I frowned. "How do you know that?"

"Oh, just a tidbit I picked up when a gorgeous swan put the squeeze on Sylvester's derriere," Matilda said. "He jumped and squealed and proclaimed he was a man of the cloth."

We dutifully followed Matilda back to the scene of the

current chaos and came upon the cat and the chipmunks in a face-off.

Trey stood in the middle, holding up his hands like a traffic cop. All he needed was a whistle. Instead, he took the mic from whom I assumed was Alvin, then in a low crooning voice, asked, "May I?"

He headed to the little black box by the platform that served as a stage, then pushed a few buttons. A thumping beat started to hum in the room, and Trey started to sway, then he began to sing. As only Trey could.

Rockin' around the Christmas Tree never sounded so retro eighties, but Trey was a singer. Not just any singer. He had his own Jon Bon Jovi tribute band he traveled with. Or did.

His intervention seemed to do the trick, and Devon grabbed my hand and pulled me out as fast as possible.

"Come on. If we don't leave now, we're done for."

We headed home to our gothic and beloved disaster. Just a few weeks ago, our house was barely livable, but after our crew quit, scared off by imaginary and not so imaginary ghosts, Devon and I figured we might as well move in and use every spare minute to update things.

We had one operating bathroom, a bedroom, and a functional kitchen. The entire first floor was stripped and ready for staining. It was livable, and it was ours, thanks to the generosity of the ladies of Luckland. I believed they were trying to move Devon and me along on our path to coupledom by purchasing the house for us. Truthfully, it was quite romantic to arrive *home* after such an eventful holiday and cozy up in our nest.

As we snuggled on the couch and I burrowed into his chest, I began to feel just a slight chill. "Dev, did you turn down the thermostat?"

"Haven't touched it, Red," he murmured. Then he shivered. "You're sure you checked, and the furnace was on, right?"

"What do you mean? You said to make sure the furnace was in, as in 'in the house.'" I was sure he had said *in*, not *on*. Yesterday, Joey, the delivery guy, had delivered the new furnace and taken the old one. I'd reported back all was well. How was I supposed to know he hadn't turned it on? "Sorry?" My apology came out as a squeak. I made a habit of trying Devon's patience and optimistically hoped he had an abundance of it.

Devon chuckled and shook his head. "I suppose that was why it was like an ice box in our bedroom last night. Guess it's back to the Inn we go, then." Devon smiled, then kissed my nose. "99 will be okay as she has a fur coat, but let's hope the *other* furries have called it a night."

CHAPTER FOUR

It was not unusual to find the ladies doing odd things at odd hours. Therefore, I wasn't shocked to see them in the lobby, sitting with a few furries in a circle on the floor, chanting and humming with the scent of incense in the air.

The minute we walked in, Marcy held up her hand. I assumed she meant, "stop where you are." So, we did. We let them hum on a bit, then Marcy stood and broke the spell before she headed our way.

"What's happening? We didn't expect you back so soon." She chuckled as she swept her arms up and down a few times, letting the free-flowing colorful fabric of her Thanksgiving dress flap like wings. Marcy was quite tall and imposing, and rather mystical. I never knew whether she was guessing or having visions. Either way, she didn't usually ask questions. She usually knew what was happening.

I raised a brow. "Don't you know?"

"Quite sassy tonight, aren't you, Pip? Is this about the furnace? Joey may have delivered it, but he's not a technician. You need to get a technician out there to install it," Marcy said.

So, yeah. She knew. I didn't need to ask how because I'd

become accustomed to her unusual psychic abilities. Marcy was adept at Tarot readings and séances, all of which I'd experienced over the last few months.

About to ask if we could have one of their rooms, though I was sure she knew that too, the front door swung open, and a breeze blew in. For one short second, the hairs at the back of my neck stood on end as I expected some sort of ghostly apparition. Even when a little figure entered, I still wasn't sure I wasn't seeing a ghost. Some of the ones I'd seen seemed eerily real.

The female figure was tiny. Seriously tiny. And seriously old. She had dressed in a woman's suit circa 1980—a retro forties look with several chains and bold colors and a hat that looked like something Madonna would wear. The woman waved a cane as she strutted in. *Strutted.*

"Marcy. Marcy Feingold, where are you?"

I glanced at Marcy, who stood as still as a statue, her mouth open. After a moment, she blinked. "Aunt Hilda." Judging by her scowl, this was not a happy reunion.

"What in tarnation is all this?" Hilda swung her cane to point at the circle of furries. "Somebody help me down."

I sucked in a small breath as I realized she wanted *down*, as in, on the floor with them.

Marcy shook her head. "Aunt Hilda. What in hell are you doing here? You can't be here."

"And why not? Who says I can't visit my favorite niece? Who knows how long I have?"

"I'm your only niece, and I plan to visit you next month in New York, where you live. Mr. Cranston must be out of his mind with worry."

"Oh, that tadpole, he's just worried about filling my room with the next victim."

Marcy sighed. "Everyone, for those who haven't met her,

this is my aunt Hilda. She lives in a retirement home in New York."

"Retirement shmirement. It's a *facility* where old folks go to die. And I'm not going there yet."

Hilda gave Marcy a quick hug, then proceeded to march back to the circle and settle herself in Marcy's place on the floor. Without a bit of help.

Hope sat directly across from Hilda. "Hilda, it's nice to see you again," Hope said.

Hilda squinted her eyes and smiled. "Ah yes, Hope. How are you, my dear? You're looking as sprite and lovely as ever."

"I could say the same for you," Hope said with a smile.

Clearly these two got along well. I didn't think I'd ever heard Marcy mention Hilda, but perhaps I needed to pay more attention.

"So, looks like we're having a group reading, then?" Hilda asked as if it were perfectly routine. She took my mom's and Matilda's hands, then nodded at the circle of furries and non-furries alike. "Okay, let's get on with it. You, Foxy." She closed her eyes. "No, no promotion, but you might want to take another look at that guy in the third cubicle. The hot one. He's got an itch for you."

Foxy shook their head and mumbled something I couldn't quite hear. I wasn't sure if they were denying what Hilda had told them or asking for more information. I, for one, wanted more information. Like, how did Hilda know what Foxy had been thinking? Did Hilda have the same psychic abilities as Marcy?

Before I could ask, Hilda turned to the next furry in line, a cute squirrel with big brown eyes.

"Hmm. Yes, you *do* need to apologize to your mother, and soon." The little squirrel put their hands over their mouth as if surprised by Hilda's accuracy.

I admit I was a little surprised myself.

Hilda continued to answer the burning questions the furries seemed to silently ask. Then, and only then, did she turn to the women, starting with my mother.

"Kate. You and your hubby are the lovebirds with separate houses. Always thought that would be a recipe for the perfect marriage. And yes, she'll wear it."

Wear it? Hilda could not possibly know my mother had been trying to get me to try on her wedding gown. I wasn't engaged.

"Tillie, glad you found your man. Yes, go on, tie that knot. You belong together."

My head spun. Hilda was beyond intuitive. Whatever psychic abilities she had seemed to blow the other ladies out of the water. I was used to Marcy being more talented in that arena than all the other ladies, but even Marcy couldn't touch Hilda's powers.

Hilda looked about then. "Where's that handsome young devil?"

Matilda smiled. "You mean Devon?"

"Devon? Pfft no. Finnigan! Where is that lovely young man."

When had she met Finn? When had she come to Luckland? I'd seriously missed out because she reminded me of Sophia on the Golden Girls. Only Hilda was Jewish, not Italian—which according to Marcy, if you're from New York, was the same thing. I was pretty sure Hilda was way older than Sophia though.

"Right here, Hilda. How are you, sweet thing?" Finn came over from the desk and leaned down to give her a kiss on the cheek. Finn, like myself, was a redhead, but a handsome one. If I didn't have Devon, and Finn liked women, we could have been a match made in heaven.

"Finn. Dump him. He's shifty, and he's got a thing on the side."

Finn's face dropped, then he shook his head. "How'd you know?"

"You can do better. Now, sit down here next to me." She grabbed his hand and pulled, forcing the entire circle to shift to let him in. He easily plopped his lanky body next to her.

"Okay, Hildy... Give it to me. Where am I going to find Mr. Right?" he asked.

"Oh, heavens no, Finn. I can't give that up. You'll miss out on all the fun of finding him."

Hilda then turned her attention to Marcy. "Come, sit by Hope. It's your turn." Then Hilda nodded directly at the furries still in the circle. "Go have a drink on me at the bar," she declared with a grin.

I noticed then how perfect her teeth were. Implants? They looked natural, but at her age, wasn't that near impossible? Maybe she had a secret. Surprisingly or not so surprisingly, the furries left, with Foxy stopping and crouching to give Hilda a quick hug and a whispered thank you before leaving.

When the circle held just the ladies and Finn once more, Hilda stared at Marcy and Hope.

"You two are hiding something from me. Come clean."

The women looked at each other, eyes wide. Was this about their upcoming wedding? The one everyone in Luckland talked about? Did Marcy not tell Hilda? Or just not invite her?

"Out with it, girls. Shall I give you a hint? I understand Le Bonne Fille in Taos now has the highest-rated cheese fondue in the Western Hemisphere. That imposter, Henri La Ponte, is up for a James Beard award. Seems he's already winning other awards left and right."

"That's impossible. Your fondue is the finest in the world," Marcy stated emphatically. Hope nodded next to her.

"When I gave you those recipes, you promised never ever to reveal them. Now it seems some of them are the talk of the internet."

"How do you know La Ponte is using your recipe?" I asked. Even though I hadn't been introduced, I decided I needed to join the circle and squeezed between Finn and my mom.

"I went to the restaurant myself to see what the fuss was about. And you must be Pippa. Kate's daughter."

"I am," I said as I nodded at my mom, who ignored everything around her as she scrolled on her phone.

"Ah, yes. You were off on a safari of some sort last time I was here. And your new boyfriend? Off playing secret agent, as I recall."

While I tried to reason how she knew who I was as I looked absolutely nothing like my pixie blonde mom, or how she knew who Devon was and that I'd decided to pair up with him, the man in question sidled next to me, nudging me to allow him to sit. He'd gone to the bar when Hilda turned up. Maybe the furries drove him away. Something did because Devon never willingly engaged in anything mystical and posse related.

"Ah, there he is now, the love child." Hilda raised her eyebrows. She was like a Luckland encyclopedia. I mean, I couldn't help wondering what she *didn't* know.

"Okay, the thing is, Aunt Hilda," Marcy said slowly as if trying to form the correct phrase. "We're all being blackmailed."

CHAPTER FIVE

"Blackmail?" Hilda sputtered. "That's absurd. What do they want?"

I had a moment, admittedly, where I wanted to ask how Hilda *didn't* know all this. All these women with their psychic abilities, yet their abilities seemed not to apply to themselves. Quite curious really. I made a mental note to start researching this quirky phenomenon.

"We don't know what they want, but a few months back, we all received threats at book club," Marcy said.

"Threats? Go on."

I sat up and tuned in closely. Not as closely as Devon. If he were an alien, he would have sprouted antennas about then. He'd been furious that the ladies refused to reveal their secrets so he could help mitigate the repercussions of someone leaking them.

"The caller alleged they knew our secrets. We'd carefully guarded our personal information for years, but as it happens, we lost track of some of it. An accidental event," my mom said.

Hilda scowled. "How did you *lose track* of your secrets?"

"There was a yard sale. Some shoeboxes disappeared. We

haven't found them yet," Hope said, glancing at Devon with a tiny frown. "Soon after, we each received a threat, so we assume whoever has a shoebox has some of our secrets."

"Like your recipes," Hilda stated.

"Well, yes. Someone leaked our cheesecake and lasagna recipes, which were in a shoebox," Marcy said."

"And now you know who," Hilda said triumphantly.

"You think Henri La Ponte has our recipes?" Hope asked. "That he's got one of our shoeboxes?"

Devon and I had figured that the person who had leaked the recipes had one of the missing shoeboxes, and it seemed Hilda had found out who.

She pursed her lips. "Well, either that or the person who has the shoebox gave the recipes to him, and the more recipes they release, the fewer tricks you two have up your sleeve."

Hope glanced at Marcy, then nodded. "Yes, it's a possibility, but it's not as if we're getting rich off them."

Hilda shook her head. "Well, La Ponte is, and we need to stop him."

I understood the value of a good recipe, especially in today's foodie environment. It wasn't just about the café, it was about branding and going wide, seeing your cheesecake in the grocer's freezer perhaps, and it was *always* about making money.

The thing was, the Luckland Ladies didn't need money. They had oodles of it after my mother and her besties took a little trip to Vegas thirty years ago and came home millionaires. So, in the big scheme of things, money wasn't important to them.

I supposed when someone ruled the roost in a small Colorado town and never wanted for anything, it was easy to thumb your nose at someone out to intimidate, but if someone were to blackmail or try to intimidate me, I'd be running to the local police chief. Then I'd jump in his lap and beg for help.

"You're going where?" Devon looked at me the following morning as if I'd lost my mind. At five o'clock, I was up, dressed, and ready to go—which wouldn't be out of the ordinary had it been summer, and I'd planned a photo hike. However, it was late November, and I typically slept in, especially as we were comfy at the Inn with actual heat.

"We're going to Taos. Last night, the ladies decided to check out that resort Hilda thinks is serving up her recipes. They said they want to plan Marcy and Hope's wedding, which will now also be your mom and Trey's, and Martin and Pru's." I held up my phone and showed him the text I'd received just before I'd gone to sleep, Devon already dead to the world beside me.

"That's too much to process, Watson. You're going to investigate a recipe theft while planning a *triple* wedding? With the entire posse? What about Dani?"

"Dani and her mom are meeting us there. They'll drive out from Tucson." Dani was my oldest and dearest friend, and she split her time between Tucson, where her parents lived, and Luckland, when she wasn't out diving the deep seas or training SEALs. The military kind.

"I don't like this idea at all." Devon sat in bed and watched me with his laser-beam eyes. They tended to get very intense when he focused on me, as if he knew there was more I wasn't telling him. There usually was. Normally, he'd insist on coming, just to keep us out of trouble, but he drew the line at accompanying the Luckland Ladies and their entourage on a road trip.

"Well, like it or not, it's happening, and I've got to get myself downstairs, or they'll leave without me. As you know, that could lead to who knows what kind of disaster." I needed to go even if I didn't want to. Road-tripping with the posse was an experience best reserved for the less faint of heart.

Sighing, Devon got out of bed, then collected me in his arms. "Stay out of trouble," he whispered in my ear before he nudged me out the door.

Once in the hallway, the murmur of voices from the lobby drifted toward me. I paused. Maybe crawling back into bed with Devon was a much better plan. Too late. My mom called up the stairway.

"Let's go, Pip. I've got your coffee in hand."

That was followed by Marcy. "And a chocolate croissant too."

She said that in case the coffee didn't lure me.

Downstairs, the women were all dressed alike. Seriously, as if they'd coordinated it. Winter spa wear. Colorful leggings with tunic sweaters and matching scarves. Well, everyone except Hilda. She wore skinny jeans, complete with a torn knee, a long sleeve Elvis T-shirt, and a knit cap tucked over her white locks. To my utter shock and dismay, Hilda and I matched. Instead of Elvis, I wore my Raskins NYC shirt. Either I had chosen to dress like a ninety-year-old, or she was quite the spry one.

It took at least a half hour to pack all our luggage into the infamous Luxmobile, as I affectionately dubbed it. A forty-foot luxury RV with every amenity known to humankind. The kind of RV I imagined Dolly Parton toured in. All the comforts of home and a few most of us didn't have even then. Considering the temperature, I was awfully happy about that.

First things first, I settled onto the couch with my coffee and croissant, then turned on the electric fireplace. I was happy to simply observe the ladies' commotion rather than participate. I was, after all, only along for the ride. At least, that was what I assumed.

In Devon's mind, clearly it was much more. I'd only just relaxed when my phone buzzed.

Devon: Txt me when you get there. No casino stop-offs.

The ladies did like to hit their favorite slots when traveling, but I was sure they were too distracted by the whole recipe theft caper to do so this time.

Me: No worries, they have bigger fish to fry.

At least, I hoped they did.

I fell back into relaxation mode, turned on the satellite TV, then tuned in to one of the morning shows.

"They're making my white chocolate mousse!" Hilda's voice was loud in the small, confined lounge area. "Turn that up, Pip."

Though the morning show aired its cooking segment, I didn't see how Hilda could possibly know what they were making. Still, I dutifully turned up the volume.

"Now, here is the secret," the chipper host declared as she sashayed around the kitchen set staged for a holiday party. Holding up a bottle, she smiled. "Frangelico. A delightful hazelnut twist to this classic dessert."

"Ha. I knew it!"

"Sorry, Hilda, but white chocolate mousse is quite a common recipe."

"Quite so, Pippa, but most use Amaretto. The trick to a perfect tasting mousse isn't almond liqueur. It's hazelnut. And there, see?" She pointed to the TV. "She's got the sliver of kiwi on top. That's mine, I tell you."

"Shh, everyone. What's she saying?" Hope faced the TV as the host turned to introduce someone.

"And here is the brilliance behind this wonderful, delectable treat. Chef La Ponte himself! Master chef from Le Bonne Fille in Taos!"

"Turn this heap around. Let's go to Denver, where they're making this show."

"I'm pretty sure it's prerecorded, Hilda. He's probably back in New Mexico by now," Marcy said.

"You better be right, Marcy. There's no time to waste." Hilda stomped a foot, then winced.

"Of course I'm right. Now let's all settle in, it's a long ride, and we need fortification." In Marcy and Hope's language, that meant breakfast. While I was perfectly happy with pastry, if there were omelets in the works, I was all in. After the disaster in the kitchen yesterday, they wouldn't want my assistance, which gave me a chance to relax. I did have a blog to work on, but it was too early in the morning for that.

"Say, ladies, what's the ETA for arriving in Taos anyway? I haven't driven there before." I liked to have a game plan, which required details.

"About five hours, no more than that. We should be there by ten. Rosa and Dani should be there by noon," my mom said. She rode shotgun, played navigator, handled the directions, and mapped stop-off points. These ladies had it down to a science, and while I didn't learn about their travels about the country until recently, it seemed they'd always had an itch for the road, as Matilda called it.

"No salt in those eggs, Marcy," Hilda stated as she came to sit by me on the couch. I wasn't sure how traveling with her would work out, but she seemed like a fun companion.

"Or onion," she said. "You have ketchup, don't you?"

I held my breath as I knew Marcy did not approve of anyone using ketchup on her omelets. Not even Hope was permitted to do that. Rumor had it that an A-list celebrity came to the café, and Marcy had booted him out after he'd doused his Denver omelet with ketchup.

"I do not, Aunt Hilda. You know better than that," Marcy said, her tone arrogant.

I looked at Hilda, who literally smirked with delight. I could tell she was a button pusher. I grinned at her and raised an eyebrow. Perhaps Hilda could afford us some serious fun along the way. I also might learn just a little more about these supersecret recipes from Hilda. Couldn't hurt to ask. I just needed to know when and how.

When I pulled out a book from my canvas bag, and Hilda's eyes lit up when she saw what I was reading, I knew we were destined to be bosom buddies.

CHAPTER SIX

"That's the newest one, isn't it?" she asked, craning her neck to see the cover. "The one about the lost brother?"

"You like this series?" Now there was a surprise. Not that she shouldn't like hot steamy murder mysteries, but I just thought women her age would frown on what some considered slightly pornographic. I liked to think of it as an essential distraction in my life, though Devon supplied that nowadays.

"Are you kidding? Boy, they make me hot just thinking about them." Hilda fanned herself with her hand for emphasis.

I was an unabashed fan of TK Moreaux, the mystery romance writer of the last decade, and it seemed Hilda was as well.

Hilda winked and grinned. "Who's your favorite?"

Each book in the series contained an incredibly hot detective. "Ambrose. Murder at the Fairgrounds. No contest." Before Devon returned to Luckland, Ambrose was my permanent book boyfriend.

"My favorite is Tate. Murder at the Chateau." Hilda wiggled her eyebrows. "He reminds me of a young man I knew back in the day. In fact, there's a lot of him in Tate."

Something about the way she said that last bit struck me, and the way she smiled...

"Hilda? Why do I feel like there's a really big secret you're not sharing?"

"Are you good with secrets?"

I sighed. I couldn't lie to her. "Nope. I suck at keeping secrets. If you tell me, you might as well publish it in the New York Times."

"More like the National Enquirer in this case, but perhaps if we get along, I'll tell you anyway."

She waited a heartbeat, but somehow, I knew. Deep down in my bones, I knew her secret. Maybe for once, I could keep it. There was something else I was dying to know though.

"Hilda, when you were answering the furries' unspoken questions, I figured you had the same psychic abilities as Marcy, so I assume it's a family trait. Granted, yours are definitely stronger than Marcy's, but I've sometimes wondered why she doesn't know the answers to her own questions. For example, we've been trying to find who has the shoeboxes, which in turn would lead to who may have leaked the recipes, but every time Marcy and Matilda, who have similar abilities, have tried to channel that question, they get no answers. Why?"

"Well, first, it sometimes doesn't work on one of our own like a close family member or friend. Marcy and her friends are too close for her to get a clear reading. Also, for my 'power' to work, the person asking the question has to already have an inkling about the answer. Otherwise, I can't get a sense of it."

"I don't understand."

"Well, take Foxy, for instance. They had already guessed they wouldn't get the promotion, and they were already aware the guy in the third cubicle had the hots for them, but they weren't sure if they should go for it or not. So, their answer to the question was already there. They just didn't know it."

Okay, I thought I understood how that worked, but... "How did you know what they were thinking?"

Hilda chuckled. "That's a little more difficult to explain. It just happens. If you project into the universe a question you desperately want an answer to, we can usually pick it up. It's not always clear, but I must admit, being in Luckland certainly boosts my abilities. There's something in the earth that just resonates power." Hilda waved her hand in the air for emphasis.

Hmm. The posse often spoke of Luckland's energy that they tapped when they did their annual Founders' Day ritual to appease the spirits. After all the increased sightings of ghosts, I wasn't entirely sure their ritual had worked this year. Though I hadn't believed in spirits and hauntings until recently, I had decided to ask the ladies if they'd thought something had gone wrong. However, the ladies had ignored my question and changed the conversation to Devon's and my relationship. Something I'd shut down quickly.

<hr>

After breakfast and a few hours of reading, I decided to satisfy another of my curiosities about the recipes. After all, that was the reason for this trip. Wedding plans? Nah, that could be done anywhere.

"Hilda, are the recipes, the ones you gave Marcy, are they yours? Did you create them yourself?"

"Actually, Pippa, that's quite the story. The recipes are awfully special to me. Let me tell you."

I laughed in response. "Please do."

"Picture it. New York, 1958."

"You're a Golden Girls fan, aren't you? Sophia always said something like that."

"Let you in on a secret; that was *my* line. Anyhoo, I was

dating a very hot Hungarian chef. Nikolai." She sighed. "We're talking sizzling. We were cooking it up, and not just in the bedroom."

I shook my head because I couldn't picture it. "Bet you were pretty hot looking back then, eh?"

"Back then? Bite your tongue, missy. I'm still hot. We started realizing our concoctions were really quite extraordinary, and he began serving them in his café in Greenwich Village. Very bohemian at the time. Not what you find today. Too gentrified. Well, sadly, my little Slavic dish ended up switching sides and dumped me for a chorus boy. I took the recipes and tucked them away. Figured if any of my other career choices failed, I could try my hand at opening a restaurant."

I narrowed my gaze at Hilda, who for all intents and purposes looked quite sincere. However, Devon had taught me to not only look beyond the surface, which I already did as a photographer, but analyze it. Something wasn't adding up.

"None of the café recipes seemed very Hungarian to me. Except the goulash. Marcy's goulash *is* to die for."

"No, we were very international and multicultural. We blended ingredients from all over. For example, my cheesecake recipe. You know cheesecake originates in Greece."

"Wait, it wasn't invented in New York?"

"Heavens, no. It's a Greek dessert. However, a few thousand years of tweaking does change things. But it was cream cheese, which is very American, by the way, that gave us the New York style. Technically, Reuben, as in the sandwich, created the recipe. Legend has it, he tried a cheese pie at a dinner party, and the rest is history."

"So, other than the cheesecake, which is delectable, what other recipes did you create that Marcy and Hope serve at the café?"

"Ha, so many. I could write a dozen cookbooks, but I

wanted Marcy to benefit from my experience. She's tweaked some of them over the years, of course. Perfected them. Not the goulash. That's original."

"So, what makes that so special?"

"Well, you see, when the meat is simmering, with the—"

The RV came to a screeching halt, and I thought we were going to tip over.

"Jesus, Prudence, you trying to kill us all?" Hilda exclaimed.

"No, but someone is," Prudence shouted.

"What?" Now I was on alert. Outside, it was just getting light. We were on the side of the road in a pullout just barely wide enough for the Luxmobile.

"She exaggerates, ladies," my mom said. "It's nothing. There was something in the road, and we simply didn't want to run over it."

"Something? What on earth was in the road?" I demanded.

"A horse. A mustang, probably. Had a beautiful black mane."

"What? He was just standing there?"

"Yep, seems so." My mom turned back around as if nothing were out of the ordinary.

When my heart no longer beat like a bass drum, I managed to take a few breaths. Prudence began pulling back onto the highway, and Hilda went right back into her story.

"Where was I?"

"Goulash," I muttered. I'd never get used to the mayhem that seemed to follow these ladies everywhere they went.

"You know, goulash is easy, but what you need to learn to keep your man satisfied isn't going to be found in a recipe."

"Who said anything about keeping anyone satisfied?"

She winked. "You don't need to say it out loud. I know."

She was kind of right. I sometimes wondered if I had the right stuff to keep Devon interested in me. Though we'd known each other our whole lives, he'd gone off to be an FBI agent while I'd become a photographer. Yes, I'd visited places around the world, but my life wasn't as exciting as his, and maybe I didn't have whatever it took to hold on to him.

I nudged her. "So, oh wise one, if the secret to satisfying a man and keeping him that way isn't in a recipe, where is it?"

"TK's books." Hilda grinned and pointed to my book that lay on the end table.

"Maybe we should stick to talking about food, Hilda." I did not want to have a conversation about sex, which predominantly featured in those books. "So, you were a chef back in the day?"

"Heavens, no. I did a bit of singing and dancing with a swing band. Even had a stage name, you know."

"Do tell!" I tried to imagine Hilda as a young Lolita type. Or perhaps more of a Lucille Ball. Hilda's hair was snow white, so it was hard to tell.

"Goldie Goodnuff."

"Goodnuff?" I snorted with laughter.

"I wasn't Doris Day, but I was good enough for Meyer to hire me. You know Meyer Davis was the king of swing back then."

When I'd finished laughing, I was about to ask her more, but Devon chose just that moment to call.

As soon as I answered, the entire RV went silent.

"Do you mind?" I really didn't need an audience.

"Mind what?" Devon asked.

"Not you, the busybodies who have suddenly dropped everything to eavesdrop."

"Tell them I'm talking dirty to you."

"Funny. What's up?"

"Are you sitting down?" He did ask the silliest questions.

"The way Prudence drives? You need to ask?"

"Guess what I found?" His voice held a note of mystery.

"A lucky penny?"

"No. Guess again."

"Devon, what did you find?"

"A trapdoor." He sounded triumphant.

"Where?"

"Mudroom."

"And? Where does it lead?"

"I don't know yet. I'm just about to go explore."

"Oh, wait a minute." I quickly headed to the back bedroom that housed bunkbeds for the women, then closed the door. "Remember the ladies attempted to dig around the house last month?" I whispered. "They said we had a ghost and wanted to dig up some bones, and we thought...you know."

"Yes, I remember, and I had that in mind when I found the trapdoor."

"Well, go! Call me back. No, wait, take the phone with you and me along with it."

He chuckled. "I'll call you back. Promise." With that, he hung up and left me hanging.

I could hardly believe it. Devon may have just located Luckland's legendary gold.

CHAPTER SEVEN

"Trapdoor at Mystic Manor," I stated quite casually as I focused my stare on each of the women while taking notes of their expressions.

They were all quiet, all eyes on me. Not one of them batted an eyelash. Not a single twitch. Not an ounce of surprise.

"And?" Matilda asked.

"*And*...none of you seem surprised. Or interested in where it leads."

I sat back and tipped my head the way Devon did when he interrogated me and waited for me to fess up.

"All old houses have quirky trapdoors and secret panels. It's nothing shocking," my mother said, her tone defensive.

"I'm sure it's just a cold cellar," Hope declared. "When they built the house, refrigerators didn't exist, you know."

"Quite so, Hope." Marcy nodded. "In fact, that's exactly where I'm sure it leads."

"Or it's a storm cellar," Prudence remarked from the driver's seat. "Weather can be frightful, you know."

"Or"—Hilda's eyes seemed to sparkle with excitement—"it's where they buried all the bodies during prohibition."

"Good point," my mom said. "Hadn't thought of that one."

"You hadn't thought of that when you were all coming up with what to say if we ever found it?" I asked.

"Whatever do you mean by that, Pip?" my mom asked, all huffy.

"Maybe it leads to some sort of gold mine," I said, then waited. Luckland was built on the legend that the four founders who settled the town had discovered gold. Every year, we celebrated Founders' Day with a treasure hunt to attract tourists who wandered around town with maps looking for the gold. Until recent events had changed my mind, I hadn't believed in either of Luckland's legends—the ghostly hauntings or the gold —but just last week, Devon and I had unearthed a record from the 1850s that the founders had registered for a patented lode claim, proof they'd found gold but not how much or whether they'd dug it up. Since then, nothing. Secret maps and tall tales were all that were left. So, finding any kind of mine would be a very big deal. From the women's expressions, however, they didn't seem to think so. Even Hilda didn't show an ounce of interest.

"Look. I know you're all hiding something. You always are." I did my best to keep my voice level and calm. "So, we'll leave it to Devon to figure out what. He said he's going exploring."

"Speaking of that wonderful boy, we think we should expand our wedding. Right, girls?" Hope grinned and winked at me.

Wow, that was a quick topic change, but there was no point in pushing the issue, so I went along with them. "Expand it how? According to the text I received last night, those of you who are unmarried are now all getting married at the same time."

"Not me," Hilda said, her tone emphatic.

"We're talking about you, Pippa," my mom said. Wow, she was skirting around some dangerous territory there.

"I believe it's traditional for the couple to actually agree to get married, as in one asks the other, 'Hey, will you marry me?'" I tried to keep the snark out of my voice, but I might have been just a tad defensive about it, as if maybe the fact Devon hadn't proposed might have affected me more than I wanted to admit. Not too long ago, I hadn't wanted to contemplate marriage. The fact my parents didn't live together had made me adverse to the idea of matrimony, but over the last couple of weeks...

"He hasn't asked?" Matilda sounded shocked.

I wasn't. "No, Tillie. I would have remembered if he had."

"Well, don't you worry about that. We'll fix it."

"No, nobody will fix anything. We are perfectly fine as we are." I glared at Matilda for emphasis. *If* Devon proposed, it would be on his terms. I did not need any of these busybodies screwing around with that. Anyway, there was no way I wanted to tie the knot in a quadruple ceremony with these crazy women. More than likely, they'd have an Elvis impersonator as the minister, the band would be someone from the Mullet Madness tour line-up, and the guests? Well, that would be anyone's guess. The ladies would probably invite their furry friends.

I hadn't thought about my idea of a wedding because I hadn't thought of getting married. Not really.

"Ladies, I do appreciate your concern. However, I'm still adjusting to the permanence of Devon in my life, and *if* we make it official, I'd want time to plan it out so I can have *my* perfect day." There, that should appease them.

"Fine, Pip, we'll respect that. For now," Hope said.

My phone rang, saving me from further embarrassment.

"Well?" I asked Devon, then held my breath. I put him on speaker so we could all hear the news.

"It's an old-fashioned cold storage box."

"No gold, huh?"

The ladies showed no reaction, and I wondered what was going through their heads. Again, I had the distinct impression they knew more than they let on.

"Afraid not, Red. But there are a few old bottles of brew in here from what I'm guessing was prohibition days."

"We can drown our disappointment in them. Save one for me." I smiled as I hung up. Disappointed, yes, but also relieved. I didn't want half the town invading my property with picks and shovels.

"Now, who can we get to perform a wedding ceremony on Christmas Day?" Prudence asked.

I silently chanted, *no Elvis, please no Elvis,* while hoping the gods of wedding planning were listening.

"Pippa, you look a bit green. Are you carsick?" My mom peered at me closely. She was usually not much of a concerned mom type, but for some reason, she'd been paying more attention to Babs and me.

"I'm fine," I answered. "I was just thinking. You know. If I knew any good ministers."

"Spit it out, girl. What were you really thinking?" Hilda asked with a smirk.

"Okay, so I was just a bit concerned about your choice of emcee for this show."

Matilda grinned. "Well, for god's sake, Pip, we're not hiring a DJ. This is my first and only wedding. My big day."

"I know, Tillie. I'm just hoping you don't go all Vegas on me with an Elvis or worse."

They all looked at me as if I were nuts.

"Elvis?" Prudence tutted. "Elvis wasn't really our thing, Pippa. We're not *that* old. Now, if you said Springsteen or ooh... Rod Stewart."

"Fine. You're not that old. I just want you to have a beautiful wedding with nothing weird going on. You all deserve a classy affair."

"And you think we can't pull that off?" Marcy looked peeved. "This is Hope's and my wedding too, you know. Our first and only."

"Excuse me, but just because it's my fourth walk down an aisle, Martin and I were destined to be together. He was my first and only true love," Prudence said.

"I get it, ladies, okay? I will leave you to your planning. I have blogging to do anyway," I said.

"Well, better hurry it up. We're almost there," Prudence announced.

"Probably a good thing. This little two-lane highway meandering through mountains is starting to scare me. Where are we staying anyway, the resort?" I asked.

"Heavens, no. We can't very well go on an espionage mission and stay hidden if we're staying there," Prudence replied. "I've got us a spot at the RV park."

"Might I remind you that the last time we frequented an RV Park, we had an ostrich farm next door and ended up with a dead body in a bus. Do they not have a Holiday Inn nearby?" I mostly muttered that to myself as nobody was listening.

"Here we are, hang on, hard right," Pru shouted.

After another five minutes on what amounted to nothing more than a dirt path between towering trees, we ended in an empty clearing save for a beat-up camper or two.

"Pru, this place is deserted," I commented while keeping my tone polite.

"It's ski season. Everyone stays up in ski valley this time of year. Here, we'll have more privacy."

Looking around, it seemed a bit *too* private. "Are there

bears? Mountain lions? Park rangers? Seems to me this is a little on the creepy deserted side, rather than peaceful and serene."

"Wait till you get out and see the view," Marcy remarked.

I frowned. "You've all been here before?"

They all looked at one another.

"Mom?" I turned to my mother, who would hopefully be an open book. She offered nothing. Zippo.

I stepped out of the RV and, looking up, caught my breath. To one side, snow-capped mountains towered above the tree-lined valley. Off to the west sat a lake, untouched and unspoiled. Soft, deep blue ripples gently lapped the rocky shore. To the south stood a wooded break of pine trees, branches dusted with white. If not for the eyesore parked in the center, it would be perfect.

The door to the aforementioned eyesore, a beat-up camper with hundreds of stickers from places like End of the Road and Area 51, creaked open. I watched with keen interest to see who, or what, would come out.

CHAPTER EIGHT

"Is that a puppet?" I whispered to Hilda, who'd come up alongside me. We were about ten yards away from the camper. I didn't want to get too near as I could smell it from where I stood. Not the most pleasant scent.

I stared at the little bald man on the steps with a very large puppet sitting on his lap. It wasn't technically a puppet. I believed they called them dummies—the life-size stuffed figures ventriloquists have. The puppeteer was very small compared to his oversized companion, who, at first glance, was neither animal nor human. In puppet terms, he was more of a caricature. I just wasn't sure of whom. The dummy had wild, curly black hair, a beak-like nose, cherry-red lips, and fins instead of hands. Maybe just fingerless hands?

"His name is Philo," the little man who held the puppet said.

Hilda elbowed me.

Then the dummy spoke up. "Yeah, toots, it's Philo."

"Hilda," I whispered, mimicking the man and not moving my lips. "Why are we out here conversing with a ventriloquist when we could be on our way to a spa?" I wasn't trying to be rude, but a hot stone massage awaited me.

"Sweetie, there's no masseuse at the hotel. I've already been. They've got a Finnish sauna, a chef who's a fraud and a thief, but no masseuse."

"You sure?"

"Damn straight. First thing I asked for when I got there last time. Left them a two-star review."

"You probably told them to bring in a masseuse, didn't you?"

"Yep. I even pulled a few up on that yeller app on my phone."

"You mean Yelp?"

"Yelp? Well, pretzel pop. No wonder I could never find a good Chinese restaurant. No matter what I needed, it always gave me a list of hot chicks in thongs."

"You know, Hilda, I kind of like you," I said with a grin.

"So, if that's Philo, who are you?" my mom asked the little man as she came over and joined us.

"Artemis Ainsley, at your service," the little man replied.

I seemed to be hung up on the fact he was little, but it was all so strange. The thing was, he had big feet. Really big feet. He wasn't wearing shoes, and his toes had to be four inches long. *Who has toes that long?* I guessed his shoe size at thirteen or fourteen, even though Artemis couldn't be more than four foot ten. The dummy must have been a foot taller. Artemis held up his dummy with his right arm, where I supposed there was a contraption in the back.

My mom went right up to the pair and started poking the dummy.

"Do you *mind?*" Philo demanded.

My mom just raised a brow and continued her examination.

"This is quite the dummy." It seemed my mom's theatre background was paying off.

"It's Philo, lady. Got it?"

"Do you have an act? Where do you perform?"

"I've performed all over the world, I'll have you know," Artemis said.

"Huh. Never heard of you," my mom said before she headed back to the RV.

Hilda and I followed suit. I didn't want to poke holes in the plans these women had concocted, but I felt it necessary to point out that if we couldn't surreptitiously arrive at the hotel in the RV, we would need transportation.

"So, ladies, how are we getting to town? If not in the RV?"

"All taken care of, Pip," Matilda said as she approached our little huddle in the parking lot. "Ah, there it is now."

I turned as one of those limo party buses pulled up—a Hummer, which could probably seat a few dozen. It was a huge machine, no less obvious than an RV. Perhaps more obvious.

"That's your subtle approach to our arrival?" I asked.

"This is a bachelorette mobile! It's perfect," Hope said.

"So that's your cover? We're all here for a bachelorette party?"

"Not just a bachelorette party, dear, a taste testing, venue selection party," Marcy stated. "That way, we can try all the La Ponte guy's recipes. See what he's up to."

"How did you plan all this in such a short amount of time?" I asked.

Hilda patted my shoulder. "As soon as I realized they were serving up my recipes, I got Finn to set up everything. I didn't need everyone fussing, so I told Finn to keep it on the down-low."

"You mean you didn't want Marcy to know you were planning to escape your retirement home," I replied.

"You could say that. Now come along. We've got a chef to take down."

The ride over was all of ten minutes. The least the driver could have done was take us around the block a few times before letting us off at the hotel entrance. The place looked charming though. Tucked between the galleries, museums, and cafés, the three-story adobe was brilliantly decorated with colorful murals along the front and sides, much like the other buildings alongside it. The hotel also looked to be a short walk from the historic plaza, making it perfectly situated for the photographer in me. I'd lately had a habit of not having my camera handy when I needed it most, but this time, I had my camera around my neck. Taos had rules about photography, but I was pretty sure that applied only to Taos Pueblo, one of the oldest populated indigenous sites in North America, which was only a few minutes away. That was where I wanted to go. The original adobe homes were said to be simply amazing.

The ladies were clearly on a mission, however, and first up was a taste session with the thieving chef. I'd never done a tasting before, so I wasn't sure what to expect. I only hoped the women would behave themselves and not get us into any situations that required extrication. They had a habit of getting us in trouble.

I followed them in, Hilda leading the way, but stopped briefly to really absorb the lobby area. The murals adorning each wall and the Vega beams lining the ceiling looked ancient. Of course, they could be an illusion, but I felt transported for a moment. I could have spent hours studying the murals. The largest one, along the side wall, was of a Taos family, clearly from long ago—a man in the distance looked toward the mountain while a woman and her child crafted a blanket. The little girl held the ends while the woman weaved, the girl looking intently at her. The mother smiled softly, almost as if humming to herself. They reminded me of Dani and her mom, Rosa—which reminded me they hadn't arrived yet.

I headed to the concierge desk to tell the ladies to wait until Dani and Rosa got there.

"But we came all this way. What do you mean he's not available?" Hilda asked.

"I am so sorry. I don't have any information other than Chef La Ponte will not be available today. Chef Harris will be handling the tasting for you. I am sure you will be quite pleased."

Someone in chef's garb approached us. The ladies might be quite pleased after all. The chef may not be our suspected foodie thief, but he filled out a chef's jacket quite well.

As Hilda huffed and turned to leave, Matilda patted her arm. "Hold up, Hilda, don't be hasty now."

Chef Harris smiled—one of those toothpaste commercial smiles. Pearly whites and all that. Then he winked.

"Well, a few minutes to see if he's up to snuff won't hurt, I imagine," Hilda said.

"After you, Chef Harris," Prudence said.

"Please, call me Monte." He held out one arm to indicate we should follow, then led us to a private room down a hallway lined with various paintings and traditional clay art pieces. The room itself was beautiful. Honestly, if I were looking for a venue for my own wedding, which I wasn't, but if I were, this would do quite nicely. Not only was it light and airy, but French doors led out to the most beautiful little garden area. Being close to winter, most of the flowering plants were dormant, so the courtyard was lined with potted poinsettias while a winter-creeper ivy with shiny green leaves adorned the walls, gripping the rough texture.

Wanting photos, I approached the chef and asked permission to snap a few while we waited for the rest of our party. He was quite amenable, and I quickly stepped outside and took a few pictures. I could have spent the day there, but we did have a charade to carry out. Plus, Rosa and Dani arrived. Finally, I had someone to buddy up with. I'd begun to feel a bit like an outsider.

When I stepped back inside, the women were engaged in a lively discussion with the chef while a server laid out fabulous-looking creations. After greeting Dani with a big hug and our ritualistic dance moves we'd created as kids, we turned our attention to the feast in front of us.

It took us an hour, but we ended up sampling every bite, and each one was delicious. I couldn't decide which one I liked most—the pastry tarts filled with spiced meat or the skewers with grilled fruit, peppers, and marinated beef.

Then Hilda leaned over and whispered to me. "None of these are ours."

I frowned. None? Did that mean La Ponte wasn't sharing the recipes with Harris? Damn.

"Chef, I must know. How is that beef seasoned? It's wonderful!" Hilda sat back in the chair and eyed Monte.

"Well, it's my own blend. Been working on it for years."

"Hmm. And why isn't it on the restaurant menu? I had dinner here just last week, and none of this was available."

"Well, I'm only here filling in for Henri, the executive chef. He doesn't permit anyone else's dishes to be served in the restaurant." Chef Harris paused, then frowned. "I made that mistake once, and he reamed me in front of a full seating. However, my dishes *can* be used for weddings if he's not in the kitchen. So, while the cat's away..." The chef grinned mischievously.

"He's a fool," Marcy stated. "This is by far some of the best food I've ever eaten."

"Agreed," Hope said, then looked at Marcy, who nodded. It seemed as if they'd just held a silent conversation.

"You know, you need a place where you can shine," Marcy said.

Monte smiled, then sighed. "I agree, but it's not so easy to find your own little nirvana as a chef."

And that was when I knew what the women were up to.

"Ever been to Luckland?" Marcy and Hope asked simultaneously.

CHAPTER NINE

"Who are you texting?" I asked Dani. We had decided to break away from the women and the wedding talk and explore the historic plaza.

"Nobody," she muttered, somewhat distracted, rapidly tapping away.

"Dani. Give me that," I said, grabbing her phone.

Simon. I should have known. He gave new meaning to the phrase "tall, dark, and handsome." Dani and he had serious sparks flying whenever they were around each other. Though Dani assured me they hadn't yet connected physically.

I scanned the text thread, stopped short, and scowled. "Okay, fess up. What's with you two?"

"Nothing at all. He appears to be spying on us for Devon."

"I don't think so, Dani girl. This seems more like spying on you."

"You think?"

"I think. This last text? OMG, girl, he wants to know what you're wearing? You guys are sexting, aren't you?"

"Not at all." She grinned, but a flush crept up her face. "I simply said it was warmer than expected. So, he wondered what I was wearing."

I handed her phone back and shook my head. Those two would self-combust if they didn't give in to their attraction.

We did some shopping, checked out a few galleries, then took her car to meet with everyone at the RV. The ladies weren't going to head right back home. Instead, they planned on spending the night in the RV, then set off early tomorrow.

When Dani and I got to the RV, we waited for the rest of the ladies to turn up. And waited. No word from any of them. We texted them. No response. After an hour or so, Dani and I knew we had to go back into town and find them. They could be anywhere, but locating seven rabble-rousing women couldn't be too hard, right?

Things did not look good when Dani and I returned to the hotel where we last saw the women. Police cars, an ambulance, and the coroner's vehicle were in front of the hotel. Not a good sign. Dani practically parked on the sidewalk in her haste. We jumped out, then ran toward the entrance, blocked by a local police officer.

"Sorry, ladies, we've got a situation in there. You'll have to wait outside or come back later. Are you hotel guests?"

Dani and I shook our heads.

"I'm looking for my mother," I said. "She and her friends were here earlier."

The man's expression changed. It went from calm and collected to suspicious. Dani and I looked at each other. Something was really wrong.

"Your mother's name?" he asked.

"Kate. Kate O'Leary."

He nodded at another officer who stepped over. I assumed it was to keep an eye on us while his partner went inside. My muscles tensed, and my nerves frayed. Someone was clearly dead. All I could do was hope it wasn't someone from our group.

Dani furiously tapped away. I figured she was texting Simon. At least, I hoped she was because, as an FBI agent, he might know what was going on. As we waited for the police officer to return, I figured the ladies had to be involved with whatever had happened. How, I couldn't imagine. We'd only left them alone for an hour or so.

Dani stepped closer and showed me her phone screen with a text from Simon.

Simon: Dead chef.

"Monte?" I asked softly so the police officer wouldn't hear me.

After a few more taps on her screen, she looked up at me. "No."

"Chef La Ponte?"

She nodded.

Okay. So, the thieving chef was deceased, but that didn't explain why my mother and her gang of troublemakers had disappeared. That was when it hit me.

Oh my god, what had they done?

My phone buzzed right then.

Mom: Hurry back. Time to go.

After a massive sigh of relief, I shook my head. *Unbelievable.* Now suddenly, *we* needed to hurry back. However, considering the current situation at the hotel, it was a great idea.

Dani and I hopped back in the car and pretty much raced out of town. Once back at the parking lot, we hitched up Rosa's car to the back of the RV, which took way longer than it should have with everyone pitching in to help and nobody having the slightest idea what they were doing. Eventually, ten YouTube videos later, we'd taken care of it.

As we settled in for the long ride, and with no explanation

from the women about what had happened at the hotel, I turned to my mother.

"Mom, what was all that hubbub about at the hotel?" Though *I* knew, I wanted to know what *they* knew.

"Hubbub? Whatever do you mean?" She raised an eyebrow, then held up a magazine with a photo of a wedding gown nobody in their right mind would wear. "What do you think of this?"

Clearly, she was pretending ignorance. Dani glanced at me, then turned to her mother.

"Mama, what was all that commotion about?" she asked.

"Commotion? Oh, I'm sure it's nothing to worry about." Rosa smiled, dismissing Dani's question. "Who were you texting earlier? Was it that luscious Simon?"

"Mama, don't. Now, about the police cars and the coroner's van. I know you know."

"I only know what I know. Now, about Simon." Rosa beamed as she said his name. She'd met him only a handful of times and insisted he and Dani were meant for each other. She said she knew these things.

Dani and I looked at each other in frustration. We were getting nowhere, so I had to use my ace in the hole.

"Well, you ladies may not be interested, but the chef is dead," I stated quite loudly as I plopped on the couch next to Dani and Hilda.

"Don't be silly. He's just taken a new job," Marcy responded. "Hope and I offered Chef Harris a position at the Inn, and he accepted."

"Oh. Well, that's very nice, Hope, but it's Chef La Ponte, the thief, who's dead," I said.

Now we had their attention. They all started talking at once, which they often did, but something seemed off about the look in their eyes. I wasn't sure if they were simply surprised or worried—worried that Dani and I might know something we shouldn't or surprised La Ponte was dead. I hoped it was the latter.

"You all didn't know?" I asked.

"How would we know something like that?" Rosa replied, her tone indignant.

"Really, Pip, the concierge said he was unavailable, not dead," Hope said.

My mom shook her head. "In fact, they could have told us that right away, saved us all some time."

I sighed. "I doubt he was dead before we had our taste testing. Someone would have called the police immediately, not hours later. La Ponte must have arrived afterward and died then."

Hilda, who had composed herself, sat upright and cleared her throat. "Seems to me we dodged a bullet, no pun intended. Maybe now our recipes will be safe again."

"Hilda, really. A man is dead," I exclaimed.

"A no-good recipe-pilfering scoundrel is dead, true, but it has nothing to do with us. So let's just enjoy the rest of our trip back. Shall we?"

I couldn't truthfully argue with that, so I sat back and tried to relax, but my phone buzzed, this time with a distinctive tone reserved for Devon.

Devon: ETA?

I glanced out the window, trying to spot the next exit sign for a clue of where we were. I thought we'd been on the road for about an hour, but I couldn't tell. I forgot to check the time when we left. Then I spotted the sign for Pueblo.

Me: Maybe 9:30.

I knew he was tracking me on an app he'd installed on my phone, so he had to know where I was. I figured he was just trying to touch base. I hoped so.

Devon: Don't get pulled over. Don't stop for any reason.
Me: ?
Devon: Just get back here. I'll explain later.

I wondered why—other than the fact the ladies might be involved with a dead chef. That would be a good reason not to stop. On the other hand... Actually, there was no other hand.

CHAPTER TEN

Pulling into Luckland on a cold, almost winter's night always seemed a little spooky—as if the town waited expectantly for the ghosts of settlers past.

What little hustle and bustle existed during the day in the small downtown area vanished at night. Partly because it was cold and partly because everything shut down, except for the police chief's office. A cubicle inside the sheriff's office was open, and that was where I requested Pru to drop me off. Dani said she and Rosa would grab a room at the Inn.

I wasn't sure where Devon and I would stay, though I hoped he had the furnace turned on at the Manor in my absence. I grabbed the few belongings I'd hauled with me and stepped off the Luxmobile straight into Devon's arms. He wrapped me in a hug but frowned as he glanced about. When he shifted me to the side and poked his head in the RV, I knew there was trouble afoot.

"Ladies, *all* of you, stay together in one house tonight. Mom, your place will do." He used his official voice. The commanding one. "Stay out of sight. Park the RV in the back. I'll be over in the morning, and we'll have a chat. Do not go anywhere, and do not answer your phones unless you know who's calling. Lock the doors. Understood?"

"Why? What's all this about?" Matilda asked.

"Not now, just do as I say." He turned around then took my hand. "Let's go." He pulled me along on foot toward the Manor.

"Devon, you do know the chivalrous thing to do is to carry my bag, right?"

He stopped and shook his head. "Sorry, Red." He quickly gave me a kiss, then smiled. "Just distracted. We've got to get home. Then we'll talk."

At least he was willing to fill me in. He wasn't always so informative, though I couldn't wait to find out why he'd told the women to all stay locked up together.

"Wait," I said. "Is our house still freezing?" I did not want his frozen toes grazing my feet all night.

He smiled. "No, it's all fixed. The house is toasty warm now. Well, aside from the drafts."

As he unlocked the door to our home, I barreled inside, flipped on the lights, and swung around to face him.

"Well? What's happened?"

Devon looked bewildered. "What do you mean?"

"Come on. Don't play with me. Obviously, there's been an incident if you made all the ladies, including Dani and Rosa, stay at your mom's. Oh my god, it's the chef, isn't it? He was offed, and you think the women did it! I knew it. They acted really weird when I told them the chef was dead."

"Really, Red, I thought I taught you better. You're jumping to conclusions again."

Right. He was right. I sighed. "Okay, then. What's the big fuss about, why did you make everyone go to your mom's house, and why couldn't we talk until we were inside?"

"Again, Pip, slow down. Now, one question at a time." He

smirked as if humoring me. Yikes. Why did men feel it necessary to humor women as if we were alien creatures?

I took a breath. Two could play this game. "Devon, my love. You seem agitated. Please tell me what's on your mind. Maybe you should sit on the couch, put your feet up, and let me get you a beer. Or perhaps a glass of wine?"

I thought he'd laugh off my sarcasm, but the stinker agreed. He literally went over to the sofa, sat down, swung his legs up on the ottoman, and leaned his head back, closing his eyes.

I, on the other hand, was left standing in the foyer, trying to figure out if I'd just been played or if he was truly that dense.

Without even opening his eyes, he spoke. "If you come on over and join me, I might have something to tell you." Then he patted the sofa cushion. I hesitated, but only for a second.

I made myself comfortable next to him, put my feet next to his in the space left on the ottoman, and leaned into the crook of his arm. Our fireplace wasn't yet up to snuff, so cuddling would allow me to steal a bit of extra warmth.

"Spill it, G-man," I said quietly. "All of it." I squeezed his arm for good measure just so he knew I wasn't only there for the intel.

"I got a call from Simon that there was trouble in Taos."

"And?"

"There was trouble here too."

"Trouble here? What kind of trouble?"

"The furries all checked out in a hurry this morning—which was odd. They'd booked two more days, according to Trey."

"Maybe they were bored."

"Maybe. But right after they left, Finn discovered someone had broken into the office in the back. Lock busted off the door jamb, papers strewn everywhere, and the computer smashed. It also appears some files are missing."

I jolted upright. "You didn't tell Hope or Marcy about this?"

"No, because I didn't need them barreling back here in a panic."

"They have a right to know. Finn will tell them if you don't. What if they go over to the Inn and discover the break-in?"

"If they go over, we'll deal with that then. In the meantime, I've told Finn not to tell them."

"You just told *me*. You know telling me secrets doesn't work all that well."

"I'm only telling you, so you understand how serious this is. My hunch says it's tied to the recipes and that dead chef."

"Monte complained that La Ponte wouldn't let him use his recipes in the restaurant. He said while the cat's away... Oh my god. Maybe the new chef offed the old one?"

"We don't know if someone 'offed' La Ponte, but who is Monte? What new chef?"

"Monte is the chef Marcy and Hope hired in Taos."

Devon's expression turned grim. "I think you'd better tell me everything, all of it, from the beginning. Do not leave out a single detail."

I relayed our entire adventure to him—except for any private discussions Dani and I may have had. Those were for our ears alone. I also didn't include any mention of wedding gowns.

Afterward, we didn't sleep much. Devon spent most of the night at his laptop, doing who knew what and chatting with Simon. Simon and Devon had worked together at the FBI. Devon had resigned over the summer to take over law enforcement in our little town. However, he and Simon still conferred, investigated, and spent way more time together than former partners would. I hadn't directly approached Devon about it, but I was almost certain he was still a Fed in some way, shape, or form. From all those spy novels I read, there must be a dozen or more secret agencies—and Devon and Simon must have worked for one of them at some stage. I kept that idea to myself though.

I pored over the photos I'd taken during the day, but I couldn't keep my mind off the dead chef. Was his death linked to the stolen recipes? Could Hilda have had anything to do with the chef's demise? She'd wanted to confront the man about those recipes, so after the chef returned to the restaurant's kitchen, maybe they had an altercation, and she'd sliced and diced him and stuffed him in a freezer. I chuckled at the visual. I'd probably seen that in a movie somewhere. Truthfully, I didn't even know if he was murdered. Maybe the poor guy just had a heart attack.

When the sun shone through the bedroom window, Billy bleated for his breakfast outside our back door. At least, I thought it was Billy. His girlfriend, Skye, was also quite vocal in the morning. The two of them ate as fast as I could feed them, snarfing anything in sight, especially anything that resembled clothing.

I headed out back, grabbed their monogrammed buckets, a gift from Marcy and Hope, and went to take care of the goats. They jumped excitedly and raced around me. For people who were lonely and needed an emotional support animal, I was quite certain pygmy goats would be perfect.

Once they were busy snarfing their food, I tidied up the shack my dad had built for them, then headed back into the house. That was when I found out we had a guest for breakfast.

CHAPTER ELEVEN

"GOOD MORNING, SIMON. WHEN DID YOU MAGICALLY APPEAR?" I asked the tall drink of water at my makeshift kitchen table, who wasn't the same one I'd left there. This one was more exotic than my nerdy dreamboat. Simon Devereaux was the epitome of southern, Cajun charm and built like one of those hunky firemen that graced the cover of every fundraising calendar ever printed.

"Good morning, Pip. I found myself in the neighborhood and thought I'd snatch a cup of coffee."

I laughed at that. "Nobody finds themselves *in the neighborhood* in Luckland, Simon. Try again."

"Hmm. Well, maybe I had a few days off? Thought I'd spend it with y'all."

I raised a brow, indicating I knew that was a bluff. He was obviously here because of the break-in at the Inn. Though why that warranted an FBI agent, I didn't know.

"I missed the goats?"

I grinned, grabbed a mug of coffee for myself, and joined him. The little table Devon and I had set up in the kitchen was more of a rickety old TV dinner tray table, but until the floors were done, we had no intention of moving in any real furniture.

"So, tell me, Simon, how'd the chef end up in the eternal ever after?" I figured if he thought I already knew, he'd spill the beans.

"Not happening, Pippa. You know better than that."

"I do?"

He grinned. "You do. Besides, we've got other things to worry about. Like keeping you and the ladies safe."

"Safe from?"

"Pippa." This time it wasn't Simon chiding me. I turned. Devon stood in the doorway, smirking.

"Come on, guys, I realize there are *details* you can't tell me, but a general discussion involving my safety warrants at least a bit of an explanation." I was going to find out one way or another but giving them a chance to tell me was worth a shot before I went off on my own to investigate.

"Just let us do our jobs, okay?" Devon was only half-kidding on that one. The problem with being Luckland's police chief is that he had to balance the law and my curiosity.

"I have an idea," I said. "Let's go over to your mom's and discuss the current bedlam with all of them. Fill them in?"

"I highly doubt they're awake. Marty said he did a drive-by at two this morning, and her house was lit up like a power plant," Devon replied with a shake of his head.

"Why was Marty driving by her house in the middle of the night?" I asked.

The two men looked at me as if I'd asked a ridiculous question, which I hadn't.

"What?" I asked, somewhat indignantly. Okay, so maybe I was fishing, but really, it was a reasonable question.

"Pippa, how about I fix some breakfast, those cinnamon

rolls you like so much, then we'll head to my mother's at a more reasonable hour."

Right, as if that was a tough decision. Three cinnamon rolls and an hour and a half later, the three of us headed over to Matilda's.

We took Devon's new SUV he'd bought last month and snuck up on the ladies. I would have thought they'd expected us. Maybe they were, but they put on a show when they opened the door yawning and stretching in their matching outfits. Not exactly matching, but they all wore leggings and t-shirts that read, "I am woman, hear me roar."

With the recent passing of one of their idols, Helen Reddy, I supposed they were paying homage. On the other hand, the shirts could have held an entirely different meaning.

Matilda tried to take charge and herd us into the living room, but Devon was in full-on authority mode.

"Ladies, if you would all please take a seat. I have some information you need to hear."

While that certainly quieted down their chatter, it also stirred their insatiable curiosity, which led to only a moment of silence before they all started in on him.

"What information, Dev? Tell us what's going on," Matilda said in a rush.

"How did that chef die, do you know?" Hilda asked. "Did they find the smoking gun?"

"Why is Simon here? Has something else happened?" Marcy and Hope looked at Dani. My guess was they assumed Dani had invited him.

Prudence lifted an eyebrow. "And what was Marty doing cruising out front at all hours?"

"Probably just wanted to see your smiling face," Hilda muttered, her tone sarcastic.

"Maybe if you'd all shut up for a moment and give the boy a

chance, we'll find out," my mother said from her perch on the sofa. She had a scone in one hand and coffee in the other, which told me they'd all been up for a while.

Devon smiled at my mother. "Thank you, Kate. Now, if you'd all be so kind as to listen for a moment, I'll fill you in."

I elbowed him softly, silently reminding him not to be snippy.

"While you ladies were enjoying your little adventure in Taos, it appears someone took advantage of your absence and broke into the office at the Inn."

Gasps sounded all around.

"Did they rob us?" Marcy was quick to ask.

"What did they take? We have virtually nothing in there, just our computer and a few files," Hope said.

"They didn't take the computer, but they did smash it. Some things were tossed about, and according to Finn, some files were taken," Devon said. "Finn discovered it just after the furries all checked out."

"The furries robbed us?" Matilda exclaimed.

"The files. They're our recipe files, aren't they?" Marcy asked."

"Ladies, we don't know for sure who did it or exactly what files they took. We're still gathering evidence. And, Mom, you say *us* as if they robbed you," Devon said.

"An offense against one of us is an offense against us all," Hope replied. "United we stand and all that."

I wasn't surprised by Hope's response. They were like musketeers—all for one and one for all.

"I bet whoever robbed you had something to do with the slicing and dicing of La Ponte," Hilda declared loudly.

"How'd you know how he died?" I asked her, my suspicions on high alert.

"Sliced and diced, chopped and dropped. I don't know how he died. It's a good way to stuff a body in a freezer though."

Everyone was quiet. So very quiet.

Hilda frowned. "What? Don't you people watch seventy-two hours?"

"The true-crime TV show is called forty-eight hours, Hilda, and of course we do." Hope smiled then. Probably in relief there was some reasonable explanation for Hilda's ramblings.

Simon put up a hand. "Okay, look. Enough about slicing and dicing, which there is no evidence of at this point. Just an unfortunate chef who's deceased. For all anyone knows, it could have simply been natural causes."

"About the robbery, we have the surveillance tape, and we'll get to the bottom of this," Devon said.

"What tape?" Hope asked.

Devon shrugged. "We might have installed a few cameras around the Inn."

"You *might* have? You mean you did. Why would you do that, especially without telling us?" Marcy asked.

"Oh, Marcy. Devon did the same for me after my house was broken into." I wasn't sure why Devon and Simon had put cameras in the Inn, but I felt I should come to their defense.

Before Marcy could respond, the door burst open, and Babs ran in, breathless or as breathless as any compulsive runner ever was. I couldn't say it surprised me to see her. She'd obviously found out about the break-in.

"Was anyone hurt?" she asked, glancing around the room.

"No, dear, but some things were broken, and files were taken," Hope said.

"One of the furries," Hilda said.

Babs's eyes widened a little as she stared at Hilda. I guess they hadn't met before.

"Marcy's aunt," I said by way of introduction. "Hilda, my twin sister Babs."

Devon's phone rang, and he took a moment to answer it. I watched him, judging his reaction to determine if the call had anything to do with the missing files, or the shoeboxes, or anything at all to do with the women. He glanced up and looked at me.

"Duty calls," he said. "I'll see you all later."

On his way out, with Simon close behind, Devon stopped to give me a soft but thorough kiss. I guess I could forgive him for abandoning me with the women after a kiss like that.

CHAPTER TWELVE

"He's here. We've got to skiddoo," Marcy declared, waving her hands toward the door.

"Skiddoo? Is that even a word? And why do we need to do that?" I asked.

"Because Finn just called. Chef Harris has arrived and is impatient to get started."

"Then you and Hope skiddoo, and we'll stay here and sort things out." Matilda began ushering Marcy and Hope out the door. Matilda had a way of becoming quite imperialistic. Generally, when that happened, she was the de facto ruler of the roost. There was always so much going on with these women that it amazed me I kept it together at all sometimes.

We all settled into our comfy chairs in Matilda's family room—the one room where we could put our feet up and kick back. Each of us had our own space and have had since forever. There was an old bean bag chair to the side of the fireplace that was mine. When I was younger, much younger, I'd grab a book and snuggle in it with a blanket. Mostly to stay out of Devon's way. It was remarkable how the years had altered my perspective. Now I'd do anything to stay *in* his way.

Dani always liked to lay flat on her back on the faux fur rug in front of the fireplace with her head at my feet while we'd chat quietly. My mother and Matilda would grab the loveseat and yak about who knew what. Hope and Marcy would always snuggle by the window seat. Prudence and Rosa snagged the card table, and Babs typically found her way to the glider in the corner. She called it her nook, but I thought it became a place of invisibility for when all the women hovered.

With Hope and Marcy gone, and everyone else so relaxed and cozy, now would be a perfect moment to ask a question I'd had on my mind for quite some time. "Ladies, I was thinking about ideas for Marcy and Hope's wedding gift, and I was wondering if any of you could tell me a bit about how they met or something, so I can work out what to get them. I'm sure they'd love something as a reminder of that time."

"That's an excellent idea," Hilda said with a grin. "Well, long story short—"

I smiled. "No, no. I want the whole enchilada, please. Deets."

Hilda nodded. "All right then, long story long... When Marcy was in culinary school, her father, my brother, didn't approve. He'd always wanted his daughter to go into show business with him, so Marcy came and lived with me, which was convenient for her as I lived just down the street from her campus, and quite frankly, I welcomed the companionship. I had just come off a difficult relationship, so having Marcy around was perfect."

Hilda paused. Noticing her glass was empty, I got up to refill it.

"Water?"

"What time is it?" she asked with a laugh.

"Ten-thirty in the morning, Hilda," my mother said. "Pip, water is fine."

I gave Hilda a sympathetic glance and refilled her glass from the pitcher on the card table. After I handed it to her, I sat back down and waited for her to begin again.

"Where was I? Oh yes, so one day, Marcy comes home in a tizzy. Some jackass at school had pilfered her notes. They were working on their final projects. Coming up with a unique twist on a traditional recipe. Well, Marcy had come up with a brilliant take on latkes—Jewish potato cakes. Instead of potato, though, she had a stroke of genius and used fruit. Then this stupid little prick stole her notes and turned in the same idea. Marcy was told to come up with something else since the instructor couldn't be sure whose idea it was. By the way, not that it matters, but that little Irish putz had no clue what a latke was until he met Marcy."

"Wait, this other student was Irish, and the instructor couldn't figure out whether Marcy Feingold came up with a latke recipe?" That was outrageous.

"Turned out that the prissy little instructor and the leprechaun were having a thing. Back then, they got away with that shit."

I don't know what surprised me more—the vitriol out of Hilda's mouth or the story itself.

"Go on, where does Hope come in?"

"Oh, that's the best part. You see, Marcy decided to do some research at the library. She asked the librarian at the desk for assistance, and in the process, told her the story. Said she was looking for a way to one-up the guy. So, the librarian went to work helping her."

"I take it that was Hope?"

"Yes, it was. Hope found a book on fruits and nutrition. They found a starchy one that would be perfect for latkes. However, it had a side effect."

"Side effect?"

"Let me tell this part!" Prudence hopped up off the sofa with a grin. "Marcy takes the information, jots down a new recipe, and leaves it on the counter during class. Of course, it somehow disappeared. The next day, they brought in their creations. Marcy had made a traditional Hungarian goulash, but with a secret twist that bowled everyone over. The pasty-faced thief? Well, he brought his fruit latkes, made with a 'strange exotic fruit,' wouldn't you know..."

"And?" I was waiting for the side effects.

"Persimmons!" Matilda shouted with glee.

"And?" I still didn't get it.

"Pip, dear, I know you aren't much in the culinary depart-ment, but certain foods have certain...properties," my mother said.

"You know the saying, beans, beans, the magical fruit?"

I chuckled. "Yes, but beans aren't exotic."

"No, but persimmons are. Now there's a magical fruit." Matilda laughed out loud. "Hope told us that the plan worked so well, Marcy's entire class had to postpone their finals until the next day because they had to fumigate."

"Then what?"

"Well, Marcy was so grateful she brought a basket of freshly baked pastries to the library the next day, but Hope wasn't there. Marcy left a note with her name, address, and phone number, and hoped she'd hear something back." Hilda smiled. "The following day, there was a package outside our door."

"First edition Joy of Cooking," Prudence said. "They went on their first date that weekend."

"They were complete opposites yet perfect for each other. Sadly, nearly thirty years ago, people weren't so accepting."

"No," Matilda said, frowning. "They most certainly weren't. Remember the time Hope called in tears? They had gone to a New Year's Eve party, and the hostess refused to let them in.

Marcy and Hope had spent their entire paychecks on new outfits, manicures, their hair... And the door was shut in their face."

My mother shook her head sadly.

"It was the social event of the year," Hilda said. "Marcy was going to try and network among *high society* hoping for a job as a private chef or to pick up catering clients. High society, my ass. Most of those people were as fake as their boobs."

"What happened after that?" I asked.

"We told them to come back to Luckland, that the café was for sale, and we knew it was a perfect fit for them." Matilda smiled broadly. The café was, clearly, perfect.

I really needed to learn more about what Marcy and Hope had experienced. Times were so different then. Then again, there were plenty of mean-spirited, horrid people in the world today, but I couldn't imagine Marcy and Hope not being together as I'd always known them. I was just about to pry a bit further when they returned, huge grins on their faces. I didn't know as I'd ever seen them so happy.

"He's a marvel," Hope announced as she and Marcy hurried over to take a seat by the window. "We arrived at the Inn, and Finn was already in the kitchen showing Monte around."

"Monte dove right in. He instinctively knew where everything would be and, in thirty minutes, had prepared the most exquisite smoked fish salad I've ever had. Monte Harris is a gem of a gem," Marcy stated as if anyone had any doubts. Of course, having tasted his food, we didn't.

"Why is he here already?" I asked. I mean, they had only just offered him the job twenty-four hours earlier. "Wouldn't he have to stick around to talk to the police?"

"If La Ponte had been murdered, maybe," Dani said. "Hope, did you ask Monte what had happened to his boss?"

"We did, and he said the police told him there was no

obvious foul play. That was why he was allowed to leave. He said the whole episode gave him the heebie-jeebies, and he needed to get away."

I wasn't so sure. With La Ponte no longer in charge, Monte might have been better off staying in the prestigious restaurant instead of a small-town café and Inn. It seemed strange he'd give that up. So, why did he really leave?

"What about the files that were stolen?" I asked.

Marcy's and Hope's happiness faded. "They were the recipes," Marcy said. "So now there are more than two people out there with them."

CHAPTER THIRTEEN

"You want to what?" Matilda drew herself up to her full height as she glared at her son, who equally postured across from her. They stood in the center of the family room, having a standoff.

Simon stood next to Devon, the object of the tense atmosphere in his hands. "As Devon explained, we need to fingerprint all of you so we can remove you from the database of prints we've taken from the Inn. We're trying to catch the perps, but we need your help." Simon had poured on the charm, but it wasn't working.

I wondered when they'd had time to take prints. Probably after they'd left Matilda's, when "duty called."

"Devon, we're just not comfortable with the idea of being fingerprinted," my mother said.

Frustration crossed Devon's face. "Why not?"

I cleared my throat and gave him a look that told him why not. The ladies were probably afraid of the Nevada authorities getting hold of their prints and linking them to the Vegas heist. I didn't see how, as the ladies had only found the bag of money, not stolen it. The money *was* stolen—by the Panello brothers, who were now behind bars but not for the theft. Instead, they were serving time for holding six of us ladies at gunpoint earlier in the year. Devon knew about the money, but the ladies didn't know he knew. After a moment, Devon sighed.

"There is no need for you to worry," he said. "Your prints will only be for me. I won't add them to any database."

I nodded. "I'll go first," I said, trying to ease the tension in the room. So began the wonderful ink session at Matilda's.

Devon and I awoke early Sunday with the intention of doing nothing but lazing about, like cuddling up in front of our non-working fireplace and sipping some hot, spiked cider. However, before I'd even gotten my morning kiss, Devon's phone buzzed. With a groan, he flung an arm toward his nightstand. After banging his hand around, he finally got hold of his phone and held it up, squinting at it.

"Shit, gotta run." He jumped up, threw on his uniform, then leaned down for a quick kiss before running down the stairs and out the front door. At least he closed it behind him, as evidenced by the loud bang.

My first thought was to worry about what might have happened. It could have been anything, of course, so I did what Devon had taught me to do, which was take a few relaxation breaths and put whatever worry I had aside. He didn't want me to agonize about him and his job. I understood there might be times he could be in danger, and I got it, but I still had to work on reducing my anxiety.

My second thought was to use the time he was at work to catch up on some photo cataloging and edit my weekly botanical blog. I'd recently gotten an amazing assignment from one of the most prominent environmental groups in Colorado who had offered me a slot on their upcoming major climate change project, so I had a fair bit of work to do.

Before that, I got totally ambitious and stripped the bed, thinking maybe I'd do some laundry. That was when *my* phone buzzed.

Mom: Matilda's, now. Hurry.

Dani: Wtf is happening? Come to Matilda's!

Matilda: I'm gonna kill that boy of mine! Come quick!

I sighed. As usual, something had gone terribly wrong, but why Devon was headed for the gallows, I had no idea. I threw the bedding back on the bed in a heap, changed into jeans and a sweatshirt, then threw on a baseball cap so I wouldn't have to braid my wayward hair.

A few minutes later, I stood on the front porch of Matilda's house, but I paused before entering. A ruckus sounded from inside—lots of shouting and stomping. Devon and Simon's cars sat in the driveway.

Babs: Get in here.

It was a twin thing. She knew I stood outside.

I opened the door to find Devon and Simon with Hilda between them. The two men looked grim. Hilda appeared resigned.

"What's going on?"

"We're bringing Hilda in for questioning," Simon said.

"Those bozos in Taos think she murdered La Ponte! And my son believes them, for god's sake." Matilda's fury was obvious.

"Did they find her fingerprints all over the cleaver that hacked La Ponte to death?" Wrong question to ask, apparently. Everyone looked at me as if I knew something I shouldn't. "Hey, I was only joking."

"Maybe you ought to quit talking, babe," Devon said.

"Maybe you ought not to call me 'babe.' Ever."

He didn't say more as they escorted Hilda out the door. As

they went over the threshold, she turned her head and grinned. She literally grinned. I knew then she wasn't guilty.

"We're going with her," Marcy said as she and Hope followed.

The moment they left, I turned back to the ladies and Trey, who I'd noticed standing somewhat awkwardly behind all the women. "All right, time to huddle up and sort this out." I thought I sounded quite authoritative. I headed toward the family room, assuming they'd all follow. Yeah, too much to ask. I ended up circling back and standing in front of them with my hands on my hips.

"Can we all regroup, get comfortable, and discuss how to fix this?" This time they followed.

Once we'd all settled, mostly in the same places as the previous day, I waited for someone else to take over, though I didn't know who. Each of the ladies was so very different, and each had a strength that presented when needed, but all of them looked too angry right then, and I realized I might have to step up.

Trey cleared his throat. "Ladies, if I may. I have a bit of experience in police procedures. We have to find out what evidence they have that would make them believe Hilda killed that chef."

Matilda smiled and looked adoringly at Trey. "Absolutely right, my love, but how do we get that information?"

Trey smiled back at Tillie. "You ask for it. It's the simplest method. They won't tell you everything, but they might give us just enough to go on."

"I think that's brilliant, Trey," Prudence said.

"Yes, of course, and I think I know who should do the asking," my mom said, looking at me.

"Oh no." I shook my head. "Devon is already ticked off at me. I really don't want to risk riling him up further."

"Oh, Pippa, he adores you," Rosa said. "You catch more fleas with syrup, you know."

"I think that's flies and honey, Rosa, but I get the picture."

"And don't forget to flash a bit."

A bit of what? Was Rosa telling me to flash my boyfriend?

Matilda jumped off the couch, practically sprinted upstairs, then returned with a shopping bag. The last time she had a shopping bag in her hand, it was filled with naughty lingerie for Dani and me to boost our love lives. The Luckland Ladies did tend to take mothering to a whole new level, but that was just their way.

Dani sat up and craned her neck to see the bag's contents. I didn't want to look. Really, I didn't, but when Dani started to snicker, that was it. I took the bag from Matilda and peered inside.

"No. Absolutely not." I looked up, horrified. "Ladies, I will do almost anything to help Hilda, but not this."

CHAPTER FOURTEEN

Whenever anyone asked me, "What's the worst that can happen?" it was a prelude to disaster. I knew this. I'd always known it, and when it was one of the posse who asked, the disaster was hydrogen bomb level.

That evening, I stood at the top of the Manor's worn and tattered gothic stairway, trussed up like a saloon dancer, complete with black fishnet stockings and thigh-high boots. I'd bundled my hair on top of my head in some sort of garter-style headwear with rhinestones.

At the bottom of the stairs stood my beloved, his face registering somewhere between shock and horror. Not the seductive grin I anticipated. That was probably because standing alongside him was a strange man in a black suit whose expression seemed to be mild amusement.

I froze because it was too late to run. A smattering of excuses rolled through my head, but only one seemed feasible.

"Oh, hello. If you'll excuse me, I'm late for rehearsal." The words came out in a rush as I dashed down the stairs and out the door—into the frigid cold. Mortified, I got in the Jeep and headed to Matilda's.

I barged in like a lunatic and raced to the back, where the women were all seemingly relaxed, just enjoying the evening. Thankfully, there was no sign of Trey.

"Well, does anyone want to know what I learned?" I asked, hands on my hips.

Dani put her hand over her mouth to cover her obvious smirk, then nodded.

"That Devon has a new friend in town."

No response.

"Devon brought said friend to the house. Unannounced."

I waited a beat.

"So, you ran," my mother said knowingly. "The question is how fast, and did he get a good look first?"

"They both did." I plopped on the bean bag chair after beating it a few times in a failed effort to fluff it back up. Or release tension. Laying back, I sighed and held up my hand in a universal gesture.

"White or red?" Dani asked.

"Don't care, just bring the whole bottle." I closed my eyes, then started to regret sitting down so low. The corset-style bodice and itchy nylon skirts were incredibly uncomfortable.

"Wait, hold that thought. Matilda, please tell me you have a t-shirt and sweats I can borrow?"

"Of course. Upstairs in the guest room."

I heaved myself up off the chair, grabbed Dani by the hand as I'd need help getting out of that ridiculous outfit, and we headed upstairs.

With Dani's help, I shed the horrid costume and got comfortable. The only t-shirt I found, suspiciously laying conveniently on the guest bed, was prophetic—a colorful image of a French cabaret scene, which I figured was just Matilda's warped sense of humor.

Dani and I headed downstairs and located the women all

gathered at the table. Rosa had a deck of cards. "What are you playing? Can Dani and I play too?" I asked.

"Skip to the Lou," Prudence replied with a grin.

"Don't you mean Skip to *my* Lou?" Dani asked.

Rosa shook her head. "No, not at all."

I nudged Dani when I saw the accessories for the game. Shot glasses and a bottle of tequila.

"I think they mean the loo," I said with a grin. "Maybe it's one of those games where you test the limits of your bladder."

"Pippa," my mother said in warning and none too subtly.

"Mom, if the shoe fits. It's like that commercial, you know, she's got poise? In her pants?" I laughed because it was funny, and I laughed even more when I remembered the ladies often complained how laughing was sometimes risky business for them.

Prudence smirked. "Someday, Pippa. Someday you'll need a bit of poise yourself."

By now, Dani was laughing so hard tears ran down her cheeks.

"Poise or not, everyone might as well take your pee breaks now because Hilda needs our help." Rosa's voice was firm, but she smiled. A good sign. "Since the simple plan for Devon's seduction went south, we'll need a new one."

We were saved from having to come up with a new harebrained scheme as Hilda barged through the front door, waving her cane around.

"What'd I miss?" she asked loudly as she strode into the room. Marcy and Hope trailed behind her.

"You didn't miss anything," I quickly said, hoping no one would tell her of my seduction calamity. "So, what happened? Why did the Taos police think you butchered La Ponte?"

Marcy shook her head, but Hilda smirked before she poured herself a margarita then sat next to Matilda on the sofa.

"The chef's wife apparently had photos of me standing over La Ponte's body. She sent them to the police, so they wanted to question me. However, your Devon"—she pointed to me—"said the photos were photoshopped. What the hell is that? The wife shopped for photos, and I get blamed for murder?"

I grinned. I couldn't help it. "No, Hilda. It means the chef's wife had photos that implicated you, only they were doctored."

"Ah. Now that makes sense. Devon was quite angry when he took a close look at the photos. He got in some expert to make sure, which is why it took so long. Simon was gonna look at the wife. Do some research or some such. Anyway, I'm free. So, anything interesting happen while I was almost locked up?"

"Nothing much. Pippa got caught dressed as a saloon dancer by some strange guy in her house." Dani sputtered with laughter.

Hilda flashed me a grin. "Pics or it didn't happen."

I was sure Devon would have taken pictures if he'd had time before I hightailed it out of there. I shook my head. At least I now knew who the stranger was—the photo expert. Though why Devon had brought him to our house, I didn't know. "So, La Ponte was definitely murdered?"

"We can only assume so," Marcy said. "We weren't given the details, but if they thought Hilda killed him, he probably didn't die of natural causes."

Something didn't add up, and I turned to the ninety-year-old woman. "Hilda, why don't you tell us some things about yourself. If Mrs. La Ponte wants you out of the way by framing you for murder, we need to figure out why. Did you know her?" I had to wonder if the wife could have done the dirty deed.

"I doubt it. I hadn't heard of La Ponte until I'd gone to Le Bonne Fille. Then I did some checking and found out about the awards he'd been winning. Maybe she didn't want me to reveal her husband was using my recipes."

That was certainly a possibility, though that would mean Mrs. La Ponte had to know the recipes were Hilda's, and even if Hilda had gone to jail, that wouldn't have stopped her from telling anyone. Still, I made a mental note to talk to Devon to see what he thought.

"Maybe someone else from your past knows her and used her to get to you," I said. I was probably grasping at straws, but something was definitely amiss. Why would someone want to frame Hilda specifically for La Ponte's murder? Why her and not Hope or Marcy, considering the recipes also belonged to them?

"Well, I guess. Okay. Well, sit back and have a drink. Here we go. We'll start with the Follies."

"The Follies? As in Ziegfeld? You were a Ziegfeld Girl?" My mom was suddenly all ears.

"Not quite. In my case, it was Feingold's Follies. A bit of a second-rate Ziegfeld, if you will. Off-off-off Broadway. My dad was a wanna-be barker. So, when I was born, I was destined to be a Feingold Girl."

"Sorry, Hilda, but I can't shake the image of Fanny Brice in my head."

"Barbara Streisand was wonderful in that," my mom said wistfully.

"Yes, Pip, exactly." Hilda smiled. "I was pretty hot, you know."

"Pics or it didn't happen." I laughed, only to be shocked when she pulled out a photo from her purse. The photo was in a sleeve and well protected. She handed it to me, and I held it closer so I could see. It was an old black and white image taken sometime in the fifties. In the picture, Hilda stood on stage. She looked like one of those Rockettes that NBC had on at Christmas. She wore a sequined bodysuit and a crystalline tiara, and she twirled what I supposed was a baton.

I handed it back in wonder. "Okay, I'll bite. Tell me more. Is that when you met the chef? The Hungarian?"

"Ah yes, you remember. Nikolai. That dear boy. So charming, so confused." Hilda shook her head. "Back then, men and women were the only relationships society openly allowed. Not that there weren't others"—she glanced at Marcy and Hope—"but they were on the down-low. So, Nikolai and I had a thing, which quickly fizzled when he met Ira Stone."

"Wow. That's a name for the books," Matilda remarked. "It almost sounds familiar."

"I don't doubt that," Hilda said. "Ira Stone went on to be a millionaire publisher of girlie magazines."

"Wait. What? Nikolai ran off with a porn publisher? I thought you said he ran off with a chorus boy."

"Ira was a chorus boy at the time, but ironic, isn't it?" Hilda shrugged as if it were no big deal. "But things got interesting after that. You see, as a chorus girl, I met my share of men, believe me. I wasn't promiscuous, per se, but perhaps a bit looser than history likes to recall."

"Oh, do go on." Dani sat upright, sipping her drink more rapidly.

"Well, one night, I came backstage after a set and found Nikolai and Ira in the dressing room closet. I didn't care, of course, not really, just enough to storm out right into the arms of a dream, who turned out to be one of Nik's old sous chefs who'd come to the show." Hilda smiled. "It was love at first sight."

"What happened then?" I asked.

"We spent three glorious months together. Then one day, I woke up and all that was left of him was a note. He was off to Paris to study some new technique." Hilda wiped away a small tear. "I never heard from him again. Broke my heart."

I think mine was breaking just hearing this.

"What was his name?" I asked.

"George. George Richter." She sighed.

Dani quickly tapped something into her phone and looked up, eyes wide, before handing me her phone.

"George Richter of Half Moon Bay," I read softly so as not to shock anyone. "Died peacefully in his sleep aged ninety-two, surrounded by family and friends. A devoted employee of Nadia McConnell, he served as her personal chef, valet, and companion for many years. Services are private."

You could hear a pin drop. Hilda narrowed her eyes as she saw us all look shell-shocked.

"What?"

Hope was quick to jump in. "Hilda, Nadia McConnell is, was, one of us. Our clan. You know? She was a Lucklander. Daughter of Winston McConnell II."

"What's that? You're a member of a clan?" Hilda appeared confused.

"Just an expression, Hilda. To be a Lucklander, you must descend from one of the four founders. I am a Lucklander, even though I was adopted. I still don't know who my biological parents were. Just that one of them is a descendant of one of the founders. Daniel Murphy."

I gasped. "I didn't know that, Hope." I knew Hope descended from one of the four founders, but I hadn't yet figured out which one. I'd done some research on the founders' family tree, starting from the oldest generation, but Daniel's line seemed to end at Nadia McConnell and Belle Chantelle. Belle was too young. So, was Hope Nadia's daughter, or had Winston McConnell II had another illegitimate child who was Hope's mother or father?

She smiled wistfully as she recognized my expression of confusion. "We don't know. We knew of the McConnells and Winston's two daughters. Nadia and Belle. Belle is the one you contacted at the IUAS in New Mexico. We have no idea if Winston had another child who could be my father or mother."

I wanted to ask her more, but Devon chose that moment to stride through the door. Talk about heads spinning. I closed my eyes briefly and prayed he hadn't brought the photo expert with him. When I opened my eyes, Devon was thankfully alone and staring at me as if I'd grown horns. We would deal with that later.

CHAPTER FIFTEEN

I asked.

Hilda raised a brow at that expression, then smiled. "Fifty-nine, as I recall. Before Marcy was born. I remember how much it brightened my spirits when she entered the world."

"Did he ever mention the McConnells? I'm just trying to figure out how all the pieces fit." I disliked coincidences as much as Devon.

"I don't think so. Where is Half Moon Bay?" Hilda asked, changing the topic's direction.

"Near San Francisco," Devon said as he sat on the floor next to me. He wouldn't fit on the bean bag chair, or I was sure he'd have nudged me off it.

"Oh my. George was originally from California. He often told me about how he missed The Painted Ladies. I remember it became a running joke. I thought he meant, you know, ladies of the evening."

"What *did* he mean?" Marcy asked.

"The homes in a particular neighborhood are colorfully painted. I'm sure you've seen photographs." Hilda laughed and shook her head. "I knew we should have traveled together more."

Marcy smiled. "I have seen photos. I just didn't know they had a name for the houses."

Devon placed one hand on my thigh as if sensing my need to get more pieces for this jigsaw puzzle of clues and half answers. There was a picture out there, but I just wasn't seeing it. I glanced at him, assuming he knew something, but he just smiled and shook his head, which was frustrating. Then, the door opened, and Simon strutted in.

Suddenly, with Simon in the middle of the room, the cozy little space became cramped.

"Ladies, Devon, is everyone present? Where's Trey?" Simon asked.

Why would he need Trey?

"Trey is at the Inn helping Finn supervise some of the work," Matilda said.

"Okay, let's get both of them here if we could," Simon said. "I don't want to have to repeat myself."

I frowned. That sounded official. What capacity was Simon there? FBI or friend? Hard to tell sometimes. I didn't believe Hilda had killed La Ponte, but even with Devon and the expert refuting the evidence, the Taos police might still have her in their sights. We'd been through something similar a month earlier when the Tucson police accused Trey of knocking off a two-bit mobster in his tour bus. I mean, the man did die, but Trey's involvement was purely in self-defense and accidental.

While Matilda called Trey to request that he and Finn come to the house, Marcy and Hope headed into the kitchen to put together some snacks. All posse meetings required snacks, even if it approached midnight. Those were the best kind of noshes anyway. That was what Marcy always said.

We didn't have to wait long because the Inn was only a few

minutes away. Trey and Finn arrived in short order. A little dusty, which made me wonder what they were doing at the Inn.

"Excuse me, guys, but what's with the powdery substance all over your clothes and hair." It really looked as if they'd been caught in the rubble of an earthquake.

"Funny story, Pip," Trey replied with a grin. "Long story short, don't mess with big spiders."

Trey sat next to Matilda and placed his arm around her shoulders to bring her closer to him. They were such a cute couple. Maybe not cute—perhaps sweet was a better word. Finn plopped down next to Dani on the floor, which brought a glare from Simon, though totally unnecessary. Simon was more Finn's type than Dani.

Simon waited for Marcy and Hope to return, and after they placed all kinds of goodies on the coffee table, they took their seats. After we refilled the margaritas and everyone was comfortable, Simon began his spiel.

"As you all know, a murder investigation is underway. Hilda, unfortunately, is still considered a person of interest."

"Devon proved those photos were meddled with." Hilda's tone held a bit of a bite.

Simon smiled at Hilda. "Yes, I know. The Taos police are not convinced, however, so you are still a person of interest in their eyes."

Everyone began chattering at once, and the questions flew.

"Why are they still suspicious?" Hilda demanded.

"Is there new evidence?" Matilda asked.

"Can she be arrested if she goes to Mexico?" That last one was mine.

"I don't know why. Not as far as I'm aware. Yes, we do have an extradition treaty with Mexico. So, no running away, please." From the way Simon bit his lip, I could tell he was trying to suppress his laughter. He glanced around the room and waited for the chatter to die down. "As Hilda probably told you, La Ponte's widow accused Hilda of being responsible for La Ponte's death, and I'm sure you're all wondering why. However, Devon and I have it handled. I'm in contact with FBI operatives down there but keep that information to yourselves. We will do everything we can to get more information, so all of you need to stay out of it. You know what that means?"

"Stay out of it?" Dani asked.

"Yes, chérie. It means stay out of it."

The endearment must have caught Dani off guard as she blushed. A very rare occurrence indeed.

"So, do I have your word?" Simon asked, waiting for some acknowledgment.

Nothing but blank expressions. Asking the Luckland Ladies to stay out of an investigation when one of their own, or close enough, was facing mortal danger? That was never going to happen. After waiting a minute, Simon sighed in frustration.

"Ladies. Do. I. Have. Your. Word?"

Another minute later, Simon shook his head in defeat. "Okay, then, I suppose that's it. We'll call it a night."

As everyone else rose to leave, Devon stood, grabbed my hand, and pulled me out of the bean bag. Dani sat up and looked leery as Simon held out a hand to her. She hesitated for a moment, probably having a mental debate about the consequences before she finally acquiesced.

"Can we all go home now?" Prudence asked, reminding us that Devon had ordered them all to stay together at Matilda's when they'd returned from Taos.

"Yes," Devon replied quickly. "However, we still don't know where the Inn thieves are or who they are. So, everyone, please lay low."

Things were quiet for the next few days. We all behaved ourselves. In fact, it was so calm and quiet in Luckland I was almost—almost—surprised when the texts started up that Thursday morning.

Mom: Pippa, I need a ride to the cabin.

Dani: Are you headed to the cabin?

Devon: Do NOT go to the cabin.

Well, of course I ignored that last one. I headed to my mom's, picked her up, then picked up Dani and Rosa from the Inn. The cabin was the last bastion of privacy for the Luckland Ladies. It had only two purposes—for a vacation to get away from everything and as a secret meeting place for the posse. I doubted anyone was headed there for a vacation.

The drive up to the cabin that sat at the top of a mountain at the end of a long, private road always took my breath away. The Rockies were always spectacular, but with fresh snowfall at the peak, majestic couldn't begin to describe the view. The cabin itself was the quintessential Alpine ski lodge set back among the pines, though *cabin* really didn't do it justice considering it had six bedrooms, six baths, and a full gourmet kitchen.

Finding the door unlocked, we strode into the imposing structure. Being the last to arrive, the room went silent. The rest of the posse sat on the floor of the sunken living room in front of a roaring fire. A Ouija board sat in the center of the round coffee table. The ominous black triangle with the little peek-aboo window sat directly in the center of the board.

"Let's go, girls, butts on the floor," Marcy called.

I was never a big fan of Ouija. It was creepy. It also had enormous scam potential. It wasn't like the little black triangle always moved around the board all by itself, spelling out some-one's fate. More often than not, someone guided it around the board with their fingers, delivering the message they wanted someone to hear. This time, however, I was fully sure some ghostly fingers would be at work. Last time the ladies had tried a séance, we'd had a Native American woman visit us. Then Morgan, the town flirt and a server at the Blue Sky Café, and Hunter, her boyfriend, claimed they'd caused the apparitions at my home so they could film the town's reactions for some sort of freelance project. We'd basically had a Frankenstein mob outside the sheriff's office because of it. Still, I didn't believe Hunter and Morgan had faked everything I'd seen or felt, and neither did the women, so I wondered what they expected to happen now.

Because I didn't have much choice, I took my place on the floor next to my mom, with Dani and Rosa to my left. Marcy and Hope sat opposite, with Prudence and Matilda on my right.

"Where's Hilda?" I asked.

"They hauled her in for more questioning," Matilda said, annoyed.

Prudence narrowed her eyes. "Yes, your little lover boy seems to need more answers."

"He's just doing his job, and you all should leave him be," I retorted. "After all, you hired him as chief of police."

"Now then, everyone, hush." Marcy straightened her shoulders, rolled her head from side to side, then closed her eyes before she placed several fingers on the little pointer. "Who killed Chef La Ponte?" she asked quietly.

Nothing.

"Who are we looking for?"

Nothing.

"Are we in danger?"

That was when the pointer moved.

CHAPTER SIXTEEN

"Ladies, ladies!" Hope got on her feet and clapped her hands. "Listen. I have an idea."

Everyone's focus turned to her—the Ouija board forgotten.

"Look. La Ponte is dead, but culinary professionals are cutthroat, and someone will step up and take his place. If whoever has our recipes sold or gave them to him, they'll likely try and sell or give them to someone else. Not to mention the recipes someone stole from the Inn. If we make them public, even those Hilda gave us, then whoever has the recipes has no hold over us. The recipes will no longer be our secret." Hope looked fierce. I nodded because she was right.

"Look, the blogosphere is something I understand, and the best way to boost the Blue Sky Café's image is to give away the recipes. But not one at a time." I thought about what would work. "Here's what we do. We make it a VIP thing. Subscribe to our website and download the recipes. I'll photograph the finished product." I wouldn't mind if I also got to eat the spoils.

"That's a fabulous idea," Marcy said excitedly. "The lowlife will have nothing to threaten us with! Wonderful!"

"Let's call it Blue Sky Rendezvous!" Matilda remarked.

"It's a bit wordy for a blog. Try to keep it simple," I said.

"Why not just Blue Sky Café?" Marcy asked.

"Because we must be clever," my mom commented.

"Yes, clever is good," I said.

"Oh, I know, Sliced and Diced," Dani blurted with a chuckle.

I wasn't sure anyone else saw the humor in it. They all oohed and aahed as if it were brilliant. I had nothing against the name, so I nodded.

"I'll just make sure it's available as a URL." I grabbed my laptop, then started looking into my domain search app. "Someone has already registered it. Let's try something else."

"Cutthroat Culinary," Hope said with a grin.

I did another search. "Nope. Taken."

"Oh, this is fun," said Matilda. "How about Burnt Edges!"

After another search, I shook my head. "Afraid not."

"The Underground Café," Prudence said.

"Nope. Sorry. Okay, the name can wait. You'll come up with something clever, I'm sure. For now, let's get busy compiling the recipes. Marcy, do you remember all the ingredients? Can you write them out for me?"

"Of course. I can get Hilda to help with some of them if Hope and I can't remember everything. We didn't always use all the recipes at the café all the time."

I smiled. "Then we'll need to schedule a photo shoot. When can you squeeze in some time to cook up some of the recipes? Not all of them need photos, but most will."

"I'm at your disposal, Pip."

"Babs, you and mom can use your decorating skills in the Inn's kitchen. Create a backdrop so nobody can tell where the photos are taken."

Babs had discovered an incredible talent for interior decorating recently, and it would keep her from sulking if we included her.

Babs stood. "Okay, if that's all for now, I'm headed home. Mother, are you coming?"

"No, dear, you go on. Draw up some ideas for the kitchen set."

Once Babs left, we resumed our planning. We didn't have much time as, eventually, the men of Luckland would figure out where we were and invade our space. There was no time to waste.

"Looks like we're all agreed. Project sliced and diced, for lack of a better phrase, is a go. Now, Matilda, Rosa, Prudence, and Dani are on Team Hilda. We need to figure out what other evidence the police might have against her, then disprove it all." I wasn't sure how, but Dani would come up with something.

"I also want to help clear Hilda, you know. She *is* my aunt," Marcy announced. "I can cook and investigate at the same time."

"No, you can't, but that's beside the point," Matilda said. "Marcy, you're the first one they'll suspect of interfering in their investigation. If you're busy cooking, we've all got a good cover."

After Marcy agreed, we all got ready to get out of there before any of the guys showed up. Once they'd figured we'd left town, the first place they'd look was the cabin. We weren't fast enough, though, as Devon, Simon, Trey, and my dad strode in. No Deputy Martin. I guessed someone had to stay on patrol back in Luckland.

"Where's Hilda?" Marcy asked.

"She's at the Inn, enjoying the Honeymoon suite."

Marcy frowned. "Who let her have the suite? I explicitly told her to stay out of there."

"Pretty sure Finn did." Trey smiled as he stepped toward Matilda. "Hey, sweetie. Did you have a nice book club meeting?"

I'd wondered what she'd told him she was doing. It seemed

we were all at book club. I wished they'd told me, especially since Devon decided that would be the moment to nudge me.

"So, what are you reading?" he asked.

"Um…" He knew I didn't attend the posse's book clubs. Only when he smirked did I realize he was kidding. That was a relief.

"I assume you all had a reason for stopping by?"

"That we do, Pip. Ladies, if you could just give me your attention for a moment, I have news."

Silence immediately fell.

"Well, do tell," Matilda commanded. "Come on, everyone, let's all take a seat and let Devon have the floor."

"Do I want to know why there's a Ouija board sitting there?" my dad asked. "You're not all trying to talk to the other side again, are you?" After the séance, I think he'd decided he'd had enough of Luckland's spirits.

I waited to see what the women would say. Typically, nothing. Dad shook his head, then strode over to where my mom had commandeered the loveseat and sat down next to her. They were such a pair, those two. She was a petite, fairy-like creature; he was a lumbering, bearded teddy bear. I loved them both to pieces, just differently.

Devon headed to the mantel to do one of his *Devon leans*, as I called them. He crossed his feet at the ankles and leaned an elbow on the mantel. I swore the only thing missing was a pipe in his hand, and we'd have had a modern-day Sherlock Holmes.

Once everyone had found a seat, Devon nodded at Simon, who stood next to him and placed a small device on the mantel.

"Please tell me that's not a cassette player," Dani remarked a tad dryly.

"Oh, but it is, chérie," Simon replied. Hmm. There was that endearment again.

"Why do you have one of those?" she asked.

"Just wait." He pushed the buttons on the player, and we all sat in rapt attention as the tape revealed a scratchy but clear conversation between Hilda and Henri La Ponte.

"*Madam, I must insist you stop calling me.*"

"*I will not, you mensch. I warned you to stop using those recipes, and you didn't listen. So now, I'll end you.*"

"*You can threaten me all you like, but you have no proof the recipes are not mine.*"

"*The proof is in the pudding, La Ponte.*"

CHAPTER SEVENTEEN

Silence filled the room—until Devon cleared his throat. "Would anyone care to tell me what Hilda meant by that?"

"That's not Hilda," Marcy said.

"Sounds a lot like Hilda to me," Simon said.

Hope frowned. "No, it's fake."

Devon tipped his head in that way he always did, which meant he was contemplating what Hope and Marcy had said. "Fake? What makes you say that?"

Marcy smiled. "Mensch. It's not a bad word, Devon. It's a good word. A mensch is someone who does good things for others. They're noble people. It wasn't Hilda. She'd never call Henri La Ponte a mensch."

"Hilda's vocabulary, when she's angry, is far more colorful," Hope said.

Devon and Simon nodded at each other as if they'd already come to the same conclusion and had just wanted our confirmation. Then they gathered their outdated equipment and headed toward the door.

"Wait. That's it. You come here and show us a tape that

suggests Hilda threatened to kill La Ponte, then walk off. You can't do that. Where did you get the tape?" I asked.

Devon shook his head. "I can't tell you that yet, but it looks like we've been sent down a rabbit hole. We'll get to the bottom of it, no pun intended. In the meantime, I suggest you all head home. Storm's moving in."

I knew about the storm, but it wasn't a big deal. We could easily bunk at the cabin. What Devon had meant was that he wanted us close. Probably for further inquisitions, as I liked to call them. He constantly reminded me they were investigations, but it didn't feel like it when I was involved.

"Right. We need to find out who could mimic Hilda's voice like that. Whoever they are probably mimicked La Ponte's voice too," Marcy said once Devon and Simon had left.

"Artemis Ainsley," I said without thinking. "The ventriloquist we met in Taos."

"Of course," said my mom. "Ventriloquism requires a very sharp ear for voices and imitating them."

"So, it seems the puppeteer has imitated Hilda to make it appear as if she's talking to La Ponte. Then he planted that tape somewhere where the police would find it," Hope said.

"The question is why?" Marcy asked. "Why is he trying to frame Hilda for La Ponte's death? Why is she a target?"

I frowned as I added a few more pieces to the puzzle. I still didn't have the full picture, but if Artemis and La Ponte's widow had tried to frame Hilda for murder, it didn't take a genius to figure the pair were working together. It would be an interesting exercise to figure out how they knew each other.

We decided to wait out the storm at the cabin, much to Devon's annoyance if the messages I received throughout the night were any indication. He still hadn't figured out that as his significant other, he shouldn't have ordered me about. He needed a reminder every so often. Of the things I cherished most, my independence was at the top of the list—which made it difficult at times when dealing with a control freak. We were still navigating that.

When morning came, I had to come up with a reasonable response to his texts without setting off alarm bells. Not an easy task.

Devon: Where are you? Still at the cabin?

Me: No, we're on the road.

He could interpret that in several ways. The primary one being that we were on the way home—which we most certainly weren't. Prudence had gone back and retrieved the RV. At some point, Devon would notice it was missing, but I figured that moment of truth was a few hours away.

When I sent that text, Matilda, my mom, and I had joined Prudence in the Luxmobile and were headed back to Taos. The others returned to Luckland to keep an eye on Hilda and make sure to keep Devon and Simon off our tail.

We'd decided it would be prudent to learn more about Mrs. La Ponte. Not that we didn't think Devon and Simon were up to the task, but men sometimes just didn't see past a pretty face. Granted, we had no idea what she looked like, but common sense told us the spouse was always the primary suspect. Not a ninety-year-old yenta, as Prudence pointed out.

With more than four hours ahead of us, I decided to start doing a little prep work on our investigation. I searched the net and found out the La Pontes had relocated to Taos from Palm Beach around April. When I checked out their Palm Beach address, I discovered their former homeowners' association had a lovely message board—an online version of the local gossip rag. Clearly, whoever ran the group had no idea how to keep it private. Anyone could access the forum, and it seemed they did. Plus, the usernames were absurd. I was enjoying the ridiculous banter just for sheer entertainment when I came across an odd exchange.

Upstairs Preacher: *Somebody ought to tell Henri's wife to stop parading around in her undergarments! Spotted her just this morning at the half foods market. When they can't stand themselves up, tuck them away, I always say.*

Chef's Wife: *Somebody ought to tell that peeping tom upstairs to put his eyes back in his head. They aren't undergarments they are bralettes. And perfectly acceptable. And my boobs are as high and tight as anyone's.*

Well, clearly, that was Mrs. La Ponte, and she thought quite highly of herself, and it seemed, dressed a bit inappropriately. Since she participated on the message board, I felt further reading was warranted.

Apt 3B: *I hear she's got a thing for the maintenance man. Wants to pluck his plum, if you know what I mean.*

Moderator: *Please remember this is a message board for community comments and conversation. A little decorum, please.*

Chef's Wife: *Oh, stuff it, Hazel, you were on here yesterday making goo-goo eyes at you know who with the crooked nose.*

Moderator: *I'll thank you to keep your opinions to yourself, or I will have to remove you from the discussion board.*

Apt 3B: *Now, where's the fun in that, Hazel, or do you just want to pluck that plum yourself?*

As amusing as the exchanges were, I could spend hours worthlessly combing them. From what little I'd seen, whatever went on in that apartment complex was probably totally inno-cent, and they just liked to rile each other up. I scrolled for a few more minutes, then something caught my eye, and I swore out loud, getting my mom's attention.

"What is it, Pip? Find anything?"

"You could say that, Mom. Or you could say I found the mother lode."

CHAPTER EIGHTEEN

Sometimes things easily fell into place, and other times, they crash-landed. This was a crash unlike any other, for it seemed that Mrs. La Ponte wasn't some young, doting, and adoring wife at all.

The passage that had my brain circuitry firing on all cylinders was quite a doozy.

Puppeteer: *Ladies, and Reverend, can you all just simmer it down? Philo is napping.*

Apt 3B: *Simmer what down? We aren't speaking out loud.*

Puppeteer: *Well, from where I'm sitting, someone sounds like they are having a Fonda Fitness workout, and it's disturbing.*

Chef's Wife: *How do you think I stay high and tight?*

Puppeteer: *Well, then, never mind and carry on.*

That last was followed by a wink emoji.

"Pippa, kindly tell us what has you sitting there gobsmacked?" Matilda rapped her hand on the armrest for emphasis.

I read the passage out loud, leaving them all simply curious.

"I think you better back up and explain, Pip," my mom said,

clearly chiding me. She usually did at some point. What better time than when I already felt like my head was exploding?

"Henri La Ponte and his wife previously lived at the Royal Palm Pavilions, an active adult residential complex," I said. "His wife, whose name is Ginger, liked to participate on their online community message board."

"Oh, those are gossip sites for sure," Prudence commented from her place in the driver's seat. "Do go on!"

"Let me read you a few tidbits," I said, then I proceeded to read the highlights.

Matilda stood and began pacing, tapping her recently manicured fingernails against her thigh. I hadn't noticed until then that she'd gone with a very sparkly theme. Very different from her usual subdued red.

"Nice nails, Tillie. Who did them?" I asked.

Matilda smiled and winked. "Hilda, would you believe?"

"You trusted Hilda with your nails?" That seemed a little risky to me. The woman tended to be a little outrageous in her fashion choices.

"Well, it was a fair trade. She did my nails, and I found out some of Hope and Marcy's secrets to have some fun with at the bridal shower."

"Tillie, it's a wedding shower. Remember we agreed to include everyone's partners?" Prudence remarked.

"Neither here nor there, Pru. The point is, we're going to have some fun with them."

"What about you and Trey, then?" I asked. "Shouldn't we have fun with you two? And Prudence and Martin?"

That was when my mom chimed in. "Oh, I agree, Pip. We'll need to plan a few activities to give everyone something to blush about."

"I think we've gone off track," I said. "We need to get back to this little online chat they were all having. Lots of clues in there."

"Agreed. Kate, take notes," Matilda commanded. "Pippa, start from the beginning and tell us everything you've found and what you think it means."

I recapped my thoughts, summarized the online conversation, and tried to analyze as I spoke. Basically, I had a conversation with myself that Matilda kept interrupting.

"Say, Pippa, how old did your lie-busting site say those two were?"

I grinned. "You mean the website that allows me to do a background check on people?" I went to the tab I'd left open. "He's fifty-seven, and so is she. And it's truth-hunting, not lie-busting, Tillie." I had to laugh though.

"You're starting to sound like Hilda," Prudence said. "Perhaps you need some of those jellyfish supplements."

I was happy to see they had kept their sense of humor for the trip because when they were annoyed, they were seriously a pain in the ass.

"Move over, Pip," Matilda said as she flipped down the table extender and unceremoniously shoved me over so she could sit next to me. She laid her tablet down and began to tap away.

"And what might we be doing, Matilda?" I asked. "Taking over the research?"

"Did you know I joined that ancestry site? Building the family tree. Anyway, they have yearbooks, and maybe we can find out where they are from. Where did that site say they lived before Palm Beach? They usually say."

I wondered how she knew that, then I remembered she'd told me she'd been stalking Trey online for years.

"Well, in this case, they seemed to have appeared out of nowhere."

"Well, no matter, we'll find them."

"What do you mean about the yearbooks," I asked, suddenly worried. "They don't have every yearbook, right? It's not as if you could look inside every one of them, right?"

"You're still sore about that band picture of you, Pippa? Don't be. We were all in high school once," my mother said, trying to reassure me. I knew that. But...

"You didn't all have a large half-page spread featuring you, sporting a tall hat and feathers, red pigtail braids, and braces, now did you?"

Matilda shook her head. "Oh dear, Pip. You know I told Devon not to do it, but you know how boys will be boys."

At that very moment, I no longer cared about a chopped-up chef and his cheesy wife. Right at that moment, I could feel every nerve in my body zapping to attention. Recently, Devon and I traveled down memory lane. I had pointed out the photo of him I'd taken and included, as his official photograph, in the yearbook. He'd pointed out one of me I most certainly hadn't approved, making me wonder aloud who had put that horrible picture of me in the yearbook. He confessed to that particular sin but didn't explain why. I made some mental notes to revisit the topic.

"Look at this, Pip." Matilda slid her iPad over for me to see, bringing me back to our mission. "Ginger Adderly. High School of Music and Art, New York, 1982."

"Tillie, there were probably a thousand Gingers who graduated from somewhere in eighty-two," my mom said, quick to poke holes in the evidence.

"How many had a classmate named Artemis Ainsley?" I asked with a smirk. I *knew* those two knew each other!

"Let me see." My mom grabbed the tablet. She looked at the screen, narrowed her eyes, then began swiping from page to page. "Holy Hot Lips," she whispered, sliding the tablet back to us.

I glanced at the screen and saw the name Henry Lapontey. I smiled at the name upgrade he'd taken. Henri La Ponte was about as French as a schnauzer. More importantly, the chef, his wife, and the puppeteer went way, way back. They had all been performers of some sort, and from the message board remarks, it sounded like the puppeteer and the wife had a thing going.

I grabbed my phone.

Me: High School of Music & Art. New York. Class of '82.

The minute my phone buzzed, I answered.

"Did you find them?" I asked. I grinned as Devon chuckled.

"I did. You see, while you were headed to points unknown, namely Taos, I had breakfast with Hilda, who, unlike my beautiful but secretive girlfriend, was happy to discuss the puppeteer with me."

"Ha, she figured who faked that conversation!"

"She's a smart cookie."

"So, tell me about Ginger and Artemis. What else did you find?"

"Oh, I will tell you—when you get back here. And you will get back here. I've sent your ride to fetch you."

"My ride? Oh, no, Kemosabe, I think not. I have to keep my eyes on the ladies. We don't want them getting into mischief."

"More than they're already doing? I told you not to interfere with the investigation, and turning up in Taos will only muddy the waters. It's safer and less stressful for me if you're all in Luckland. So, any moment now…"

I sighed at the flashing blue and red lights and the woo-woo of sirens. They really were overkill.

CHAPTER NINETEEN

WHEN DEVON SAID HE'D SENT "MY RIDE," HE MEANT HE'D SENT SIMON as an escort to ride alongside us and ensure we took ourselves back to Luckland. Nothing like heading home with nothing to show for it. Not even a day in Taos taking more photos. However, he did bring Dani, who boarded the RV and rode back with us. I assumed that irked Simon because I knew he enjoyed her company.

"Dani, whose idea was it to reenact some sort of movie chase scene?" I asked.

"You know, I'm still trying to figure that out. One minute I was enjoying a tall stack at the café, catching up with Finn, and the next minute, I was in the passenger seat of Simon's SUV. I asked where we were headed, and he told me we were doing you and Devon a favor."

"And you didn't ask what the favor was?"

"According to Simon, he and Devon are handling things regarding Hilda, and if we went to Taos, we might get in the way. Also, *we* all have a wedding event to plan, and we should be, ahem, grateful to them." Dani shook her head. "Men," she said with an eye roll.

"I really don't get it. Neither is technically involved in the investigation in Taos. Well, maybe Simon could be, but that seems unlikely." I thought it highly unlikely. Knowing those two, they were working within the gray areas of the law. I'd always thought Devon was by the book, but when it came to the ladies, Devon and Simon seemed willing to bend the rules, and for that, I couldn't complain.

"Simon's right, girls," Matilda announced as she took a seat next to Dani and redirected the subject. "You do have a wedding to plan."

"I'm sorry, Tillie, but isn't it *your* wedding to plan?" I asked.

"Naturally, as the bride, I will be planning, but you are the bridesmaids."

"Yeah, but doesn't the Maid of Honor do all the work?" I referred to my mom, who seemed absorbed in her iPad. After Matilda got one, they all got one. They were never without them anymore. Prudence used hers to craft Pinterest boards about aliens. Matilda had used hers to follow Trey on social media. Hope and Marcy used theirs to study how to create YouTube cooking channels. Mom used hers to plan my wedding. Ever since she married off Babs to Tom, or at least took credit for it, I had been the target of her wedding fever. It didn't matter that I wasn't engaged or even in a relationship at the time.

Thankfully, Dani was in a planning mood. "Tillie, who have you chosen to perform the ceremony?"

"Colin, of course!"

"My dad? The guy who's allergic to church?" My dad wasn't fond of religious ceremonies.

"Pip, you don't have to be religious to conduct a wedding ceremony. That's ridiculous," my mother said. "Though your father is an ordained minister."

"Excuse me?" I thought my mouth stayed open on that one.

"Got his certificate last week through an online class he took at the Universal Church of the Four-Leaf Clover or some such thing."

"The one where you put in your name and address, and if you spell it all correctly, you pass the test?" Dani asked with a snort.

"Don't be silly," my mom said, her tone haughty. "He had to answer two questions correctly. Obviously, that was a piece of cake as he's quite brilliant."

Images of my dad dressed in a red and green sweater, performing wedding rites for three couples on Christmas Day, each with a unique flavor, went streaking through my brain: Matilda in a sleek white satin gown and Trey in black tie attire. Prudence fluffed out in a debutante-style gown with bouffant hair alongside Martin in a western-style suit with a bolo tie. Marcy in a colorful Sari-like garment next to Hope in her signature pencil skirt and silk blouse. I shook my head.

"What's wrong, Pip?" My mother looked at me. "What are you imagining?"

"You don't want to know. Do you have photos of the wedding gowns? I need to plan photo sessions for everyone."

"I do." My mom smiled, genuinely this time, and slid her iPad over to me. I was, for lack of a better word, stunned. I handed it to Dani, who reacted as I did. Stupefied.

"Mom, these are stunning. I mean, oh my god 'where did you find them' stunning." The dresses weren't white, poufy, or ridiculous. They were elegant satin gowns, colored with a hint of forest green sparkle in the bodice, in keeping with Christmas, I supposed, with sweetheart necklines and three-quarter sleeves that hugged instead of billowed. The photo showed all four women in the dressing room at our local boutique in Luckland.

"I can't believe Dory had anything like this in the store," I said, astonished. Not that our local boutique didn't have classy attire, but these were remarkable.

"Dory made them," my mother said with a smile. "Before she opened the shop, she was a designer."

"But these are exquisite, Kate," Dani declared. "Why would she stop?"

"Well, as you know, life happens, and life happened to Dory." That was all my mom said. Another mysterious Luckland tale to be told. Someday.

"Want to see what you two will be wearing?" my mom asked, wiggling her brow. After my recent saloon costume debacle, seeing what they had in store for me would be prudent. I nodded and closed my eyes while she searched for the photos on her tablet.

"Okay, girls, you can look."

Dani and I leaned in together and gasped. For once, my mom did well. We would look good in the dresses.

"Will the Inn be ready?" I asked, worried about the extent of renovations still going on.

"No, not at all, so we have a better idea."

"Which is?"

"We're going to use the town gazebo. Put some space heaters in, and it will be perfect." My mom had a dreamy look on her face.

Dani smiled with the same dreamy expression. "Oh, that will be stunning. Twinkling lights strung all about. Oh, and some of those propane firepit tables. It'll be gorgeous."

I frowned. "How many guests are there?"

"Well, I told the girls to each limit their list to twenty-five. So, all told, with family and guests, under a hundred."

"That gazebo won't hold a hundred people."

"It's a big gazebo, but we can flow out into the street, and as half the town will be there, though uninvited, nobody will care." My mom smiled triumphantly.

Dani smiled as well. "So, the staff at the café and Chef Harris will be on catering duty. Colin is performing the ceremony. Babs, Pip, and I will handle setup. What about music?" She loved a good party, especially if she could get out there and shake it up on the dance floor. Together we made a pretty good team—after a few shots. Though usually, we were at a club and surrounded by perfect strangers.

"That's the best part." My mom grinned—the big broad kind that revealed some of her younger self. "Trey has lined up some of his friends to play."

"Not those guys we saw at Mullet Madness?" I smirked, remembering how Matilda finally found Trey at a Mullet Madness eighties festival in Nebraska. Trey up on the stage was one thing, but the guys playing with him were livin' the dream.

I wanted to ask a question about flowers, but then my phone went off, which I automatically answered.

CHAPTER TWENTY

"What do you mean that was Hilda's parole officer?" Matilda had come over and joined us as soon as she heard my colorful exclamations.

"I mean exactly that. The woman said she was calling to check on the whereabouts of Hilda Feingold and had reason to believe she was visiting her niece in Colorado."

"Where did she get your phone number?"

"Well, I couldn't very well ask when all she did was want me to confirm that Hilda was here. Seems she thought I was the niece. Well, she called me Marcy, so there is that."

"Pippa, you lied to her parole officer?"

"No. She said, 'can you confirm,' and I said yes. Not a lie."

My mom nodded in approval. "Well done."

"I thought so," I remarked quite smugly.

"If we didn't have that damn cop on our tail, I'd pull over at the next exit so we can regroup," Prudence commented.

"He's a federal agent, Prudence, not a cop," Dani said.

I'd almost forgotten Simon had been escorting us back. Being in the Luxmobile often felt as if we were in an entirely different world. The soundproofing level was quite remarkable.

We rode the rest of the way in relative silence, each of us lost in our own thoughts, which I assumed were about what Hilda might have been on probation for. Maybe that was why she was automatically a suspect for murder. Did Ginger know about Hilda's criminal past? Maybe that was why Ginger and Artemis tried to frame her. There had to be a connection between Hilda and the Palm Beach Trio, but when I thought back to our time in the parking lot when we ran into Artemis Ainsley, Hilda had shown no spark of recognition. So, if she didn't know him, how did he know her? Through Ginger? The chef?

Frustrated, I couldn't wait to get back to Luckland to find some answers.

"No." Devon used his authoritative tone.

"What do you mean, no? If she's on parole, she's a criminal. It makes sense."

"I mean, no, she's not on parole."

"Then why did her parole officer call me?" I suddenly had a terrible hunch I knew the answer.

Devon grinned. "Really, Pip. Are you this gullible when someone calls and tells you your car warranty is up?"

"It is?" I thought I had another year.

"Or they offer you a fun-filled all-expenses paid seven-day vacation in Bora Bora for half price?" He was laughing at me now.

"I didn't end up buying it," I mumbled.

"Pippa, there are scammers in this world. I keep telling you not to be so trusting. It's like you fell off the milk cart yesterday."

"The what?" Now I was laughing. Devon often got his idioms mixed up.

"All I'm saying is Hilda has a clean record. She's never been arrested or convicted of any crime. Someone was fishing for information, and you gave it to them." Now he was getting a bit snarky. So okay, he had a point.

"Sorry?"

He smiled. "Apology accepted. I've got dinner in the oven and an hour to kill... So, what do you think we should do in that hour?"

I leaned in to give him a kiss. "As adorable as you look right now, Dani is on her way over." That made his smile, and his dimples disappear rather quickly. Devon sighed. It was just the way of things in Luckland. Privacy was hard to find and harder to hold on to.

Neither of us moved very quickly when the doorbell rang as we were locked in a heated gaze. After a few gratuitous raps, the front door opened.

"Hey," Dani muttered as she slipped into the kitchen. I should have taken her slightly apologetic entrance as a warning.

"Yoo-hoo!"

Devon rolled his eyes and shook his head. "In here, Mom!"

I couldn't say anyone was surprised when Matilda strode imperially into the kitchen, followed by her ladies-in-waiting. I wished just once they could go about their business individually rather than in a weird wolf-life pack.

"I see the horde has arrived," I murmured softly.

"Pip, dear, don't be snide. This, what you see here, is a bridal party." My mother gave me a sidelong look, then placed a large tote bag on the table. That terrified me. Either they'd brought food, alcohol, or perish the thought, more lingerie.

"Does Devon need to leave?" I asked, perfectly serious. He laughed out loud, which had my body humming.

"Don't be ridiculous, sweetie," Matilda said. "We come bearing gifts."

I bit back a smile. "That's what I'm afraid of."

"Hilda had a wonderful idea. We're going to have a scavenger hunt." My mom grinned and gave a little wiggle.

"Mom, we've got a murder to investigate, a triple wedding to plan, and a house to renovate. You want us to drop everything and go scavenging?" I tried to keep the laughter out of my voice.

"Okay, it's not really a scavenger hunt. It's a private investigative retrieval mission. We've got to get the evidence that will help prove Hilda is innocent."

Just then, Hilda made her grand entrance, waving her cane and strutting like a peacock. "Pair up, everyone. Let's go. If we work in teams, we'll get this done that much faster. Devon, you and Pippa head to Palm Beach. Dani, you and Simon head to Taos. Kate, Matilda, and Prudence head to Sedona to see Lali. I feel she'll have some insight. Marcy and Hope will handle things here. I'll have Rosa babysit me."

"Wait. First of all, none of you are going on an investigative anything, and what makes you think anyone can find anything to exonerate you, Hilda?" Devon asked, his tone a little shocked.

"The proof is out there, and we need to find it because I don't like people thinking I'm a murderer."

"You're not a murderer, Hilda. The Taos police only have you as a person of interest because of the doctored photos and some odd accusations from Mrs. La Ponte. I doubt you need to go to such lengths to prove your innocence."

"What about that tape, eh?" Hilda asked, her brow furrowed. "That sounds like I'm threatening to kill La Ponte."

I sat up with interest because, with the impromptu trip, I

hadn't had a chance to ask Devon about the tape's origins and his belief in it.

"I explained that Simon and I don't believe it's real," Devon said.

That was good, but... "Do the Taos police believe it's real?" I asked.

Color splashed Devon's cheekbones. "We never sent the tape to them."

Matilda gasped. "You didn't?"

"Well, no. It was obviously a setup, so there was no need to put extra pressure on everyone."

"Isn't that illegal to not hand over evidence?" Prudence asked. "I mean, you were upset when Matilda stole evidence from that dead body in Tucson."

"This is different. The tape was sent to my office. If whoever sent it, and before you ask, we don't know who, wanted to implicate Hilda in murder, then they sent it to the wrong person. They should have sent it to the Taos police, but they didn't, which makes me think there's something else going on."

I frowned. "What do you mean."

Devon sighed. "The recipes from the Inn. The fake Henri on the tape said there was no proof the recipes weren't his. So, let's assume whoever made that tape already knew La Ponte wanted to make sure there were no other copies of the recipes. What if, before his death, La Ponte got someone—"

"One of the furries," Hope said.

Devon nodded. "One of the furries to steal the recipes, so if Hope or Marcy claimed the recipes were theirs, they had no proof."

"I think we can all agree Artemis made the tape. So, you're saying he knew the recipes La Ponte was using weren't his and that La Ponte hired someone to steal the recipe files. When La Ponte died, Artemis decided to point the finger at Hilda, even though there was no proof La Ponte was murdered at the time. We still don't know why Artemis and Ginger would want to accuse Hilda, but the tape may answer why someone went to a lot of trouble to take those recipes." That made sense to me, and when Devon grinned, I knew he agreed.

"Well, that makes it doubly important to find out why Artemis and Ginger are trying to frame me. We have to clear my name because if my reputation is brought into disrepute and the media find out Marcy is my niece, the bad press could send the café and Inn out of business," Hilda said.

Everyone nodded, and after a moment, Devon sighed. "What do you want us to find on this mission?"

In answer, she walked around the room, handing each team a printout with the necessary information. She then went to the doorway, nodded, turned, and left.

Devon looked down at the paper in his hand, his forehead wrinkled.

"Let me see," I murmured over his shoulder.

"Later. Pack your bikini. We're off to the beach."

CHAPTER TWENTY-ONE

"Devon, are you sure it's safe to have Martin keep an eye on Hilda?" It was a little late to ask as we were sitting on the plane taxiing for takeoff.

"Of course. Did you really want me to turn down first-class tickets to Palm Beach?" He smirked and raised his brows.

"Devon, really?"

"No, not really. Look, Pippa, if we didn't go on this wild-goose chase, I'm sure Hilda would have. It's best she stays in Luckland. I trust Martin to keep her safe *and* out of trouble."

"Well, I suppose, and I've never flown first class." I grinned. "So, what are we supposed to be looking for in Palm Beach? Maybe I can get a head start while we're en route."

He reached into his inside jacket pocket and drew out a folded piece of paper.

I took a look at what Hilda had written, then frowned. "She wants us to go to Royal Palm Pavilions? That's where the La Pontes and Artemis had lived."

Devon did not look pleased by my announcement. "That can't be a coincidence. I thought you hadn't told her about the message board or that Artemis, Henri, and Ginger had stayed there."

"I didn't. I swear. One of the posse must have." I sighed. I should have realized they'd tell her, but that didn't explain why we were headed to the complex. "What does she expect us to find? It's not like they live there now."

"Her note said to talk to the source."

What kind of cryptic clue was that? "Who is the source?"

Devon shrugged. "I guess we'll find out when we get there."

We should have discussed it more, but the wonderful flight attendant serving mimosas distracted me. Seemed we would get one when we boarded as a welcome. Then after we were all buckled in and cruising at thirty thousand feet, we would get another, and another, until we landed. I loved first class.

Devon looked at me with a gleam in his eyes. "Bottoms up," he said with a wink.

He clinked his glass with mine, then leaned in to give me a kiss. After a rather heated moment, we pulled back and gathered our wits because we weren't aiming to become members of the mile-high club anytime soon.

Sudden turbulence startled me. Grasping his hand, I leaned back and shut my eyes. Devon chuckled before he murmured in my ear, "No worries, I've got you, Pip."

***

We pulled up through the circular drive lined with palm trees and parked under the elaborate portico, where the bellman quickly greeted us. The hotel Hilda had chosen for us to stay at seemed high-end and had a wonderfully colorful Caribbean appearance. Part Spanish, part African, the elegant structure had an enormous veranda and arched entryway painted sunflower yellow. I really wanted to start snapping photos.

"Marks," Devon said to the bellman.

"Yes, right this way. Let me take those bags." The driver had set our overnight bags on the pavement, which the bellman quickly retrieved. Fidelio, his nametag said.

"Devon, have you stayed here before?" I kept my voice low as we were a few steps behind Fidelio, who was tall and muscular and belonged on the cover of a hot and steamy beach novel.

"Nope, first time."

"Then how did you know just to give him your name?" I asked, confused.

He smirked and shook his head. "This is a five-star property. That's how it's done."

"Well, seems you've stayed in one or two of these before." I raised a brow. "Or maybe you watch too many episodes of Dallas."

"Dallas? That's like from the seventies." He chuckled.

"Miami Vice?"

"Eighties."

"All right, have it your way, 007." I gave up, knowing he wouldn't give me a straight answer.

"That's Marks. Devon Marks." He winked, and I grinned. I could see him slipping into the Bond role so easily. Well, maybe he wasn't always quite as debonair, but he sure as hell was just as gorgeous.

We followed Fidelio into the lobby and up the grand staircase in the center leading to a catwalk. I assumed the hotel must have originally been a home—a grand villa of some sort. The soaring ceiling in the lobby had a beautiful fresco depicting a mermaid rising from the turquoise waters. It was simply amazing. After following Fidelio to what appeared to be the far wing of the building, we entered our suite. I stood still for a moment, taking it all in. Not over the top lavish or ostentatious, the room was simply and serenely beautiful.

Sheer voile curtains donned the multi-paned arched windows and the richly stained wooden canopy bed. The bamboo and greenery throughout gave the room a warm tropical feel, and the bathroom held a clawfoot tub and a walk-in tiled rain shower. I felt as if I truly stood in paradise.

"Well, I suppose we should unpack and relax. Too late to start hunting now," I said with an exaggerated sigh, as if I cared about the hunt. In reality, I wanted nothing more than to strip down and soak in that tub.

"Oh, no, not too late at all," Devon replied with a smirk. "As I said, first class all the way, which means just leave the bags, the staff will unpack everything for us, and we can start our search now."

"I'm not sure I want anyone touching my things, Devon. It's quite creepy. I can unpack my own things. On second thought, I don't need to unpack anything. It's all organized in my bag, and I don't like putting my things in hotel drawers because I never know what's been in there."

He quirked an eyebrow and looked at me curiously. "What are you imagining was in the drawers?"

"Barney," I murmured, biting back a grin. Barney was Matilda's purple plastic portable *massage* tool. Her "companion" before she found her long-lost Trey.

Devon burst into laughter—a deep, baritone, silky smooth laugh that raised my temperature. His laugh was quite a different reaction to when he first learned of Barney's existence.

"Fine, we won't have the staff unpack," he said, swiping a tear from his eye. "So, let's head to the Royal Palm Pavilions and look for the source."

I nodded, wondering who Hilda could mean by the source.

"Won't we stick out like sore thumbs? We're not quite old enough to live there."

"We're scoping out a place for a friend."

"Good to know. How far is it from here? Can we walk? It's beautiful outside." I looked forward to the warm weather. Colorado in late fall got quite cold.

"Other side of town, I'm afraid, but the hotel has a car and driver at our disposal."

"You know this how?"

"I read about it on the plane while you were off in mimosa la-la land."

"I was not off in la-la land. I was just enjoying the ride."

"Well, try to stay awake for just a bit longer. Then we'll come back and have dinner and relax."

I nodded and grabbed a light sweater just in case the weather turned cool. Then we headed out to *explore*.

We pulled up to the Royal Palm's main entrance. Nothing about the place was what I envisioned. It was, as Devon said, on the other side of town. In Palm Beach terms, the low-rent district. Still on the beach, but not what anyone would describe as swanky. There were two palm trees out front in need of an arborist. The building itself was old and possibly ready for condemnation. What I thought may have once been a charming entryway was now simply worn and tired. It was similar in style to our hotel, with the wide veranda and arched windows, but it hadn't had the benefit of upkeep. I wasn't there to judge, but I hoped the inside was better than the outside.

Considering the place looked semi-abandoned, I was surprised when an elderly man came down the rickety-looking steps to open the car door. The Royal Palm's logo adorned his red vest, the gold buttons about to pop. His uniform appeared five decades old and three sizes too small.

He opened the passenger door, and I stepped out as Devon leaned forward to speak to the driver.

"Can you wait in the parking lot?"

The man nodded.

As our bellman went around to open Devon's door, I tried to study the older man covertly. The Florida sun had weathered his skin, the lines betraying his age. He had to be well into his nineties, but he had a kind face. Trustworthy. I wondered if he lived there or just worked there.

"Both, ma'am," he said suddenly, looking over at me.

"Damn. I said that out loud, didn't I?" I smiled as a blush crept up my face.

"Yes, you did, but no worries. My late love Gladys did it all the time. She was what they nowadays call unfiltered."

Devon walked around to stand next to me, then he placed his arm around my waist and gave it a squeeze. "My girl's the same," he said with a grin. "I'm Devon, by the way. This is Pippa."

"I'm Sean," he replied, grinning as well.

It seemed Devon becoming besties with the immortal bellman was designed to put him at ease so he'd trust us and let us wander around. At least, I hoped so.

"Just visiting?" Sean asked as he led us inside.

"Actually, yes," Devon replied. "My gram intends to relocate and asked us to look around."

"Well, it's a comfortable place. Not much on the outside"—he pulled open the main door—"but wait till you see the inside."

CHAPTER TWENTY-TWO

"I don't know as there's anything available at the moment, just a handful of vacation rentals," Sean said as I gazed in wonder at the ridiculously aging interior.

"Oh, like on one of those condos-for-rent websites?" I asked, hopeful Sean might tell us more.

"Something like that," Sean said. "It's where celebrities come to hide out without getting tailed by the media. I could tell you some wild stories!"

Devon grinned. "Celebrities, eh? Like whom?"

"Tyler Whiplash, for one." Sean nodded for emphasis.

I had to purse my lips to suppress a monstrous laugh from escaping, hoping Devon would do the same.

"Then, a few years back, that Canadian gal, you know, the one who can belt out those high notes and break glass? She was here too. And earlier this year, TK Moreaux stayed here."

"Seriously?" I'd suspected Hilda and TK were one and the same. Now, I was positive. Also, if Hilda had stayed here, then she might have already known about the message board. So perhaps the posse hadn't told her. However, if Hilda had been here at the same time as the La Pontes and Artemis and seen the messages between the puppeteer and the chef's wife, then she would have told Devon, wouldn't she?

"Scout's honor. I have her autograph to prove it."

"Her? Moreaux is female?" Devon frowned.

"Why are you frowning, caveman," I retorted. "Of course she's female."

I turned my attention back to Sean. "Wait, you have her autograph?"

"Sure. I make all the celebs sign in. Tell them it's a security log."

"Is it?" Devon asked.

"No, but I get lots of autographs that way." Sean snickered. For an old guy, he sure was a wily one.

"I'd love to see that log. I bet it's awesome," Devon said.

"That it is," Sean replied. He then looked about the empty lobby. "Okay, all clear. If you follow me, I'll give you a sneak peek."

Devon and I stole a quick glance at each other, and if I read him correctly, he had a plan to see who was here at the same time as the puppeteer, the chef, and his wife.

We followed Sean behind the main lobby counter and into a small office, where a guest book sat on the desk for anyone to see. I had to think quickly as I intuitively knew Devon wanted me to distract Sean. I turned back toward the office door and peered out.

"Did you lose something?" Sean asked.

"No, I thought I saw somebody at the counter. Maybe I was wrong."

"Oh dear, let me go and see. I can't be neglecting the residents." With that, he stepped back into the lobby, and Devon quickly began leafing through the book and snapping pictures. That way, we could spend time checking who had stayed there once we were back in the privacy of our hotel room. I kept my eye out for Sean, and when I saw him heading our way, I waved a hand in the air. Devon shut the book and stuffed his phone back in his pocket.

"Well, whoever it was has gone about their business. Now, where were we?" Sean asked, quite unsuspecting.

"You were going to show us your autographs, but you know, I swear I noticed a tiki bar on the beach." I pointed to the door that led outside to the beach area. "I could sure use a cold one about now."

Sean grinned. "Well, isn't that a fine idea. I'll be your server. We don't have any other wait staff at the moment."

"How long have you worked here, Sean," Devon asked. I could practically see wheels turning in his head.

"I started here just after I arrived. I came over with a traveling troupe of step-dancers. This was years ago, of course. Had a gig in New York, we did. With the Feingold Follies."

I stopped short. That was a tsunami of information. Devon stopped too, but only long enough to take my hand and tug me along, not wanting to alert Sean that anything was amiss.

"That sounds like quite the tale, Sean. You'll have to tell me about it over a pint," Devon said.

I was reeling. Sean was clearly our source—the one Hilda sent us to talk to. Now all Devon and I needed to do was find out why Hilda wanted us to speak with Sean. Did she believe Sean might have a story to tell that could help point to La Ponte's murderer? Did she suspect Artemis and Ginger? Of course she did. I mean, why else would they have tried to frame her if they weren't somehow involved in La Ponte's death? I almost rubbed my hands in glee. I loved it when more puzzle pieces fell into my lap.

The tiki bar, or what I supposed the residents of the Royal Palm *considered* a tiki bar, was little more than a rickety wooden structure beneath a palm tree with a few picnic tables scattered in the sand. I wished I had gloves because I could see splinters just waiting to happen. No one else was about, leaving Devon and me the only ones enjoying happy hour.

Sean went around to the back of the bar and pulled up a few frosted glasses. Interestingly, it seemed they took better care of the bar service than the tables. "What's your pleasure, miss," he asked, one brow raised.

"Whatever you have is fine." I figured anything complicated was a bad idea. "I'm just going to take a few pictures. It's beautiful down here." I waved my arms to encompass the beach. A few tall palms dotted the sand, and the deep-blue water lapped at the shore. The sunset colors that streaked the sky were spectacular, but a nod from Devon made me realize he wanted shots of Sean as well. Easy enough. Win-win.

"I'll take the same," Devon said as he took a seat at the table least likely to collapse.

Sean filled the frosted mugs with beer, then carried them over to the table, only losing perhaps a third of the contents.

I took a few shots of the shore then of Sean before heading over to the table, where we all took the first sip of our beer. I grinned as Devon and Sean ended up with foam mustaches.

"So, you were a dancer?" Devon asked, which was his way of pumping for more information.

"Step-dancer, if you will. Surely, I was itching to come to America, and if dancing was my ticket in, I took it."

"Must have been exciting, dancing on the big stage in New York City and all," I said, hopefully with enough enthusiasm to keep him talking.

"Oh, quite. Though not so different from Dublin. Noisy and crowded. Where are you folks from?"

"A little town in Colorado, Luckland. You know it?" Devon asked, his tone innocent.

"Do I? The luckiest town in the west, at least according to my sources."

Now that got even more of our attention.

"Really? I was born and raised there, yet I'm still waiting for my pot o' gold." Devon laughed and reached out to squeeze me. "This here is as lucky as I've been."

"Then you've been very lucky," Sean said. He smiled, then held up his mug and finished the contents. Checking our glasses, he grabbed both then made off to the bar for refills.

With Sean distracted, Devon turned to me. "Who is TK Moreaux? You know, don't you?"

"Our sponsor," I said with a wink, causing Devon's eyes to widen.

Sean swayed toward us with the sloshing mugs. I swore he must have been double-dipping behind the bar.

"So, who are these sources? Other folks from Luckland?" Devon asked Sean as the man set the half-empty mugs on the table.

"Well, you didn't hear it from me, but we had a guest here, oh, early spring. Steppenhoof or something like that."

Jonathan Steppenhoffer? I almost choked on my beer. I glanced at Devon, who barely kept from reacting.

Sean didn't seem to notice. "Anyhow, Steppengoof is down here one night and babbled about some legendary gold in Luckland. I remembered Hildy had also said something about Luckland. She had a niece. Marigold, I believe, and she served up Hilda's super-secret recipes at the blue... Blue Moon? Well, that had Henri and Ginger from 2C hanging on every word."

I frowned. "Wait, Hildy told Henri and Ginger about the recipes?"

"No, no, no. She'd left before Steppenloof arrived, and she never socialized with residents. She told *me* about the recipes, and I told Steppengoose. Well, him, Henri, Ginger, and the dummy. I think the reverend was there too."

So, Hilda didn't know Ginger and Artemis stayed here at the same time she did. Neither did she use the message board. So, the ladies *must* have told her, and that must have been when she decided Sean would be a good source of information. Why she couldn't have asked Devon to phone Sean, I didn't know. Granted, Hilda did like a bit of cloak-and-dagger drama. What Sean said also explained how Ginger and Artemis knew the recipes were Hilda's, which was why they'd targeted her for La Ponte's murder.

Sean paused, took a swig, and went right on. "Truthfully, we were all a little snookered, so I can't quite recall who said what. Everyone started talking at once about secrets and gold and money to be made. I remember thinking this Luckland is one lucky place. Maybe I should go someday."

I noticed the more Sean drank, the thicker his brogue.

"Oh, one last question, Sean. You and TK, I mean Hildy, were you especially close?" Devon posed the question with his elbow on the table, chin in hand, as if he were just fascinated. Truthfully, he was—we both were.

"Oh, that's a story for another day." Sean grinned, winked, and set down his mug. "Who's hungry?" He looked from me to Devon. "I know the perfect burger bar."

I could only hope it was in better shape than the tiki bar.

CHAPTER TWENTY-THREE

"Do we really have to go back?" I floated luxuriously in the claw foot tub, occasionally blowing bubbles off the palm of my hand. My eyes were half-closed, my head resting on the pillow-laden bamboo tray—the one in all the five-star hotel photos. Lit candles sat on the windowsill, and Devon sat on the bench at the foot of the tub, fully dressed and reminding me this was all only temporary. He had my robe, well, the hotel's robe in one hand, slippers in the other, and a grin on his face.

"Afraid so, Pip. You know what they say about all good things."

"No, what do they say? Isn't there an exclusionary clause for just these circumstances?"

"Sorry, Watson. It's time we head back. Besides, if you spend any longer in there, you'll wrinkle up like an alligator."

I sighed. Just the thought of returning to Luckland burst my fantasy bubble of Devon, me, a five-star resort, warm breezes, and the sway of palm trees. Devon was right though. We'd stayed one extra day already, and our phones were blowing up with texts from the posse.

Devon assisted me out of the tub, and I wrapped myself up

in the luxury robe before I sat on the massive bed and slid my hand over the satin duvet. I hated to say goodbye to it all.

"Just remember that Hilda needs our help, and maybe leaving won't be so hard." Devon's voice was laced with humor rather than guilt, so I smiled and stood, ready to face the world.

I looked about and noticed all my things had disappeared. "Did you really pack everything?"

"I was just helping you along."

"Did you consider I need to wear more than a robe on the plane?" Looking at his face, I bit back a grin. "I thought not." I placed both hands on his hard chest and leaned up to give him a kiss. "Do we have just a few minutes to kill? I want to take a few more shots of the water at sunset. On the ritzy beach. I want to compare them later."

"A few minutes, Pip, then we have to go. The driver is waiting downstairs for us. The posse is waiting for us as well."

"Oh, pay them no mind. Eventually, the texts will stop."

"You can hope so. They're mostly about you anyway."

My head spun around so fast I thought I'd pass out. "What? What do you mean, about me?"

"Well, it's your phone, so..."

"Hey, put it down, Curious George. A little privacy, please." He thought nothing of picking up my phone and reading personal texts. "Have you been pretending to be me? Answering my texts?" He'd been known to do that too. So had Dani. Those two could be incorrigible at times. "Just put the phone down and help me find a pair of jeans and a sweater so I don't die of hypothermia when we land."

"No worries, I'll keep you warm," Devon said, eyes twinkling.

I gently but firmly shoved him out of the way so I could access my bag and retrieve my clothes. Once dressed and ready, I grabbed my bag and camera, and we headed down to the lobby. Devon gave me five minutes for photos, which he made a big show of by using the stopwatch feature on his phone. I went out the rear entrance to the veranda that overlooked the ocean and snapped away as quickly as I could. The sunset was spectacular, a descending fireball leaving trails of orange and purple mixed into the clouds dotting the sky. I sighed, knowing the photos would be wonderful, but I wasn't here long enough to do justice to a blog entry. Maybe I could write about wanting to return.

⁂

"What's that in the bag? I do hope you brought some of that Royal Palm's brew I've had a yen for," Hilda said as soon as Devon and I entered the cabin the following morning. She sat on the floor in the middle of a circle with everyone else who'd already returned from their tasks, including their significant others. Babs was also there, though Tom was absent. In the center of the large circle were several items.

"Sorry, just airplane snacks," I said as I placed my bag and coat on the side table in the entry, then headed toward the circle, Devon close behind. We took a seat between my mom and dad. I tried to make sense of the objects in the circle. A book, a candle, and a thumb drive. Seemed to be meager findings for such an extravagant fact-finding mission.

"I'm afraid we didn't bring an object back. Were we supposed to?" I asked.

Hilda shook her head. "Information is just as important." Then she turned to Simon and smiled. "Why don't you tell us what you and Dani found."

Simon reached into the center of the circle and grabbed the book before holding it up. "Murder at the Chateau, by TK Moreaux," he stated with an emphasis on the author's name as he stared straight at Hilda. *He knew.*

"Where did you get that?" Hilda asked, raising a brow.

"The restaurant. Le Bonne Fille. The book was sitting right there at the prep station in the kitchen as if someone deliberately left it there for us. I don't like setups, as you well know from that phony tape."

"Maybe it was just a coincidence," Hilda said before she sighed. "For those of you who don't know, I'm TK Moreaux. I wrote the book."

I doubted it was a coincidence, but I couldn't see how one of Hilda's books left at the restaurant had anything to do with La Ponte's murder. It wasn't as if anyone working at the restaurant knew she was a suspect—unless Ginger had left it there as another way to keep Hilda at the top of the suspect list. She probably had access to retrieve her husband's things. Though how would Ginger know Hilda Feingold was TK Moreaux? Unless Sean had told them the same night he'd told them about the recipes. It certainly wouldn't take the police long to figure out Hilda and TK were one and the same.

"Did anyone tell you anything interesting while you were there? Perhaps who the book belonged to? I assume if no one claimed it as their own, that it belonged to someone who no longer worked there," Devon said.

Simon smiled. "I did ask, and the consensus was it belonged to La Ponte or Harris."

"Well, it couldn't have been Monte," Hope exclaimed. "Monte has dyslexia. He hates to read. He told us that when he asked La Ponte to show him something, La Ponte would tell Monte to look it up, but Monte couldn't really understand what he was reading properly. Especially recipes. He's self-taught, you know."

"Are you sure?" Simon asked, causing us all to gasp. Nobody ever questioned Hope. He'd learn that soon enough.

"My good man, you may be a professional investigator, but I've spent my life with readers, and I know when someone has trouble. I've made it my business to learn so I can help them. In fact, I've promised Monte to do just that. There are ways to help those who have dyslexia, you know."

"My apologies, Hope," Simon said. "You make a valid point."

"Has everyone read the book?" Hilda asked. "Raise a hand if you haven't." Nobody did. "Well then, the significance of the book should be clear."

I frowned. "That a chef is murdered?"

Devon leaned over and whispered, "It's not what, Pip, it's how."

"But no one knows how La Ponte was murdered yet. Or do you?" He hadn't told me he'd gotten the report, and I assumed he wouldn't get one considering the murder wasn't in his jurisdiction. I should have known better.

"Devon, maybe you could share how that miserable thief died?" Hilda requested.

"Technically, asphyxia."

"Strangled?" my dad asked.

"Anaphylactic shock," Simon replied. "He had allergies serious enough to kill him."

"That's how I killed off the chef in the book. So now you all think I did it, don't you?" Hilda was angry. "I'm not that stupid, you know. If I wanted him dead, I'd have done something completely different."

"Exactly, Hilda," Devon said gently. "We know you didn't murder him, but we've had two people trying to frame you. We have to ask how they knew you're TK Moreaux, what makes them think you would have a reason to kill La Ponte, and whether either of them had the chance to leave the book at the restaurant if it's not the dead chef's?"

I glanced at Devon. Considering how loose-lipped Sean was, there was a good possibility Jonathan, Ginger, Artemis, and the reverend knew Hilda was TK, but Ginger and Artemis were probably the only ones who had reason to kill the chef if my assumptions they were having an affair were correct. Ginger would know Henri had allergies, and she would also have the opportunity to leave the book at Le Bonne Fille. We needed proof though.

"Let's shelve that for now," Simon said as he laid the book back down. "So, what's with the candle?"

I wanted to know that too. It was obviously used. The wick was black, the wax uneven at the top.

Matilda picked up the candle. "As you know, we went up to visit Lali in Sedona to have a reading with her. This is the candle that burned during our session. As you can see, it was a very short session."

"I'm assuming Lali is a psychic," Devon said. "Why would you need to go and see her? Don't you do psychic readings, Marcy?"

"I do Tarot readings, which is a little different, but sometimes we can't see problems and issues that surround those emotionally close to us." She indicated those seated around the circle. "I've tried with no luck, so Hilda thought it best Kate, Matilda, and Prudence see Lali. She's very gifted, and certain... energies in Sedona help with her talent."

"Okay, but why do you need the candle?" Devon frowned, which I'd learned was his impatient frown.

My mom threw him a deadly glance. "That candle is loaded with leftover psychic energy. It will help us understand the deeper meaning behind La Ponte's death. If we know why someone killed him, we can figure out who." She sat up a bit straighter, then looked about the group. I thought she might have been waiting for someone to challenge her. That would be me, naturally.

"Well, Mom, don't keep us in suspense! What did Lali say?"

"She told us to look back in time, and there will lie your answers."

Back in time could mean anything. The La Pontes and Artemis knew one another from way back. The recipes were cocreated in the fifties by Hilda and Nikolai, her hot Hungarian chef. Jonathan Steppenhoffer knew Prudence from the eighties, and he also knew of the café and its super-secret recipes, but he was now in jail for another murder, so I thought it unlikely he'd orchestrated La Ponte's murder, though considering he'd hypnotized poor Prudence to believe aliens had landed on Earth, who knew?

"Go on," Hilda said in encouragement.

"It means whoever killed the chef—it wasn't anyone in this room," Prudence said.

"Oh, for pity's sake. We know that. Can you all just get to the point?" Deputy Martin sounded frustrated. He was typically such a laid-back guy. I rarely heard anything snarky from him.

I watched as Prudence gave him a quelling glance, patted him on the arm, then continued. "Certainly. It means we can narrow down our focus."

I noticed every man in the room rolled their eyes. Once again, Lali's answer seemed clear as mud, and until something triggered a memory or a situation occurred, nothing would make sense.

Marcy cleared her throat, then raised her hand, palm out, to ensure she had everyone's attention. "We all know Hilda is not capable of hurting even a tiny insect unless it's a spider, but I'm not sure if a spider is technically an insect. In any case, that leaves Ginger, Artemis, and possibly one of the furries."

"Seems obvious to me it's the widow. She probably detested her husband," Hilda said.

I smiled. "Let's not forget she and Artemis were clearly more than old high school chums."

"Well, that might mean the puppeteer had a motive as well," Rosa said. "You know, jealousy is a lover's worst enemy."

Dani smirked. "Mama, you saw that man in Taos. Did he look like the murdering spurned lover type?"

"You know love is blind. The heart wants what it wants." Rosa darted a glance at Simon, then back to Dani. Rosa clearly saw what we all saw between the two of them.

"Regardless of motive, they tried to frame Hilda, so they're definitely at the top of the suspect list. Once Devon tells the Taos police what we've found, I'm sure they'll pull Ginger and Artemis in for questioning," I said.

Devon nodded in agreement, reached into the circle, and grabbed the thumb drive. "Is this from the café?"

"Yes," Marcy said. "How did you know?"

"You aren't the only intuitive one in the room, you know," he replied with a chuckle. When everyone turned to look at him suspiciously, he held up a hand in apology. "Okay, fine. Finn told me he gave it to you and Hope. I assume your mission was to ask the staff if they'd seen anything suspicious over the last few months?"

Marcy nodded. "Well, yes. Originally, we kept the recipes under lock and key at the café, but since we moved the café to the old bakery and started renovating the Inn, we transferred all our files to the office there because it was bigger. Hilda wanted to know who knew we now stored the recipes at the Inn, so we asked the staff if anyone had been asking odd questions or acting shady."

Devon nodded. "Finn remembered something and checked the security footage for the café. He went all the way back to early spring and caught sight of La Ponte and his wife dining in the café several times, during which the chef wrote in a small notebook. Finn said if you zoom in you can see he's writing down ingredients."

"So, wait, La Ponte got the recipes by eating in the café?" Hope sounded incredulous. "He guessed the ingredients?"

"Maybe. We still have to find out why and who stole the recipes from the Inn," Devon said.

"Well, I know which furry," Simon said with a grin.

My mom huffed as she waited for Simon to explain further. "And?"

"Sylvester. When we checked the Inn's footage, we caught a man on camera sans costume breaking into the office, but the picture wasn't clear. However, we picked up some white fibers from the office, and we eventually found the same fibers in one of the rooms, which Trey told us he rented out to the cat. We don't know who Sylvester is at this time because he signed the Inn's register as John Hancock, which is obviously a false name, so now we're relying on the prints to come back with a match to someone."

"The *priest* stole the recipes?" Matilda exclaimed. "You can't trust anyone, can you?"

"You can trust *some* people," Simon said. "There is one more thing I should mention. We found out why all the furries left in a hurry. It seemed odd they'd all leave the same night Sylvester broke into the office, so once we knew which furry to blame, we contacted some of the others." Simon glanced at Marcy and Hope. "They all claim they saw several ghosts. One in particular. The Scarlet Lady."

"Oh. Well. She does seem to be active a little more than usual," Hope said. "Nothing to worry about. Wanting to see ghosts is why most folks come to stay at the Inn." Her tone was dismissive, but she'd straightened her shoulders, and I didn't miss the little flick of her eyes toward the rest of the posse.

"Have you seen her?" I asked. The Scarlet Lady was one of the more notorious ghosts the Inn was famous for.

"Me? No." She glanced at Marcy, and I could guess Marcy had seen the ghost, but there was something more to the story, I was sure. I was about to ask, but Devon chose that moment to give me a slight nudge.

"Pip, why don't you tell everyone what we've found."

Now there was a shocker. Devon including me as an equal? As a capable investigative partner? My heart grew tenfold. I glanced over to make sure I heard him correctly. His gaze was direct, sincere, and oh so swoon-worthy I could only smile idiotically—like a besotted sixteen-year-old.

I put aside my question about the Inn's ghosts and focused on how to explain what we'd found. What we'd learned would impact everyone in the room. Particularly Prudence. Devon's job involved far more than just solving cases. Every case had victims, and he had to give details to those victims, details that could hurt. Not just to strangers but to friends and family, and it was a wake-up moment for me. Still, if he trusted me, I would do my best.

"Devon and I went to Palm Beach, as you all know. By the way, Hilda, exceptional accommodations."

Hilda grinned, thankfully back in good humor. "I suspected you'd enjoy them."

"We met a very nice man there. Named Sean. Ring a bell?"

Hilda's grin grew even wider. "You found him."

"That we did," Devon said. "Quite a fellow."

"That he is," Hilda declared.

"Sean was gracious enough to share some stories with us," I said. "I assume when you found out Artemis and the Le Pontes had stayed there, you thought it would be a good idea to talk to Sean?"

Hilda nodded. "He's full of information. I was sure he'd know something about them, but as you've no doubt realized, talking to him over the phone wouldn't have given you all the details. He's a much better storyteller when he's had a few drinks under his belt." She smiled wistfully as if remembering some of his wild tales.

"He definitely had information about the trio, and more. He told us they had a visitor after you left, another renter in the vacation condo. I'm not sure the name will be familiar to you, but it is to the rest of us." I paused, took a breath, and plunged in. "Jonathan Steppenhoffer."

I looked at Prudence. The room grew so quiet I could have heard a pin drop.

Martin appeared exceptionally tense as he also looked at Prudence. "*The* Jonathan Steppenhoffer. The man who murdered your first husband and had a hand in killing your second?"

"That's the one," Pru replied quietly.

"You know whenever anything bad happens, Jonathan isn't too far behind," my mom said.

"Go on, Pip," Prudence commanded. "Tell us all of it."

"It's a bit convoluted. I'll try to make sense of it for you. Jonathan seems to have tied on one too many at the bar on the beach. Sean, Artemis, the La Pontes, and another resident they called the reverend, were all with him. Jonathan told them the legend of Luckland's gold."

There was a collective gasp. I had their attention now, for sure.

CHAPTER TWENTY-FOUR

"So, you see, it was like the telephone game, only out loud and all at once. Everybody yammered on about something in Luckland, like the gold, the café, and the recipes. We believe they were all hungover and confused the next day, but it seems Ginger and Henri remembered enough to head to Luckland in search of treasure."

"It's also quite possible the reverend is our priest, Sylvester." Devon just couldn't resist getting a word in.

While Devon and I were still in Palm Beach, Simon had rung us and confirmed Sylvester had broken into the Inn's office, which was when we'd discussed the probability the reverend and Sylvester were one and the same. It seemed the group agreed because no one batted an eye.

"Do you think Sylvester stole the recipes for La Ponte? You know, no copies, no proof they didn't belong to him. Do you think the furry thief is linked to the murder?" Prudence asked.

Devon nodded. "It's certainly possible. He would have had just enough time to get to Taos, and it's feasible he knew about La Ponte's allergies. So, we need to focus our attention on Ginger, Artemis, and Sylvester the furry."

"So, how do we catch them? What's the plan?" Matilda asked.

"Well, now we know what we're looking for, I say we set a trap," Hilda announced.

"*We* don't. This isn't a game of Clue. One of them is a potential murderer, and y'all need to settle down and let Devon and me do our jobs," Simon said, holding his hand out like a stop sign.

"I'm going to have to back up Simon on this. You need to let the law handle it." Devon was in authoritarian mode—which was always great for our love life, but truly horrible in a room with the posse.

"Devon, my boy, we're in it up to our eyeballs, and with or without your help, we shall figure this out." Matilda's voice brooked no argument, and I, for one, thought we should exit while we could—before the ladies started making plans.

Unfortunately, Devon's phone rang, and within minutes he made his own exit with Simon and Deputy Martin. My dad and Trey followed moments later.

"Um, did they leave any vehicles behind? How are we supposed to get home," I asked.

"Don't worry," my mom said just as Prudence pulled the Luxmobile around front and blared what always reminded me of an air-raid siren.

Babs, who'd pretty much remained silent throughout the entire yak fest, finally spoke.

"I am *not* getting on that thing. I'm calling Tom to pick me up."

"Sorry, Babs, but this time you are not abandoning us. One of us goes, we all go." As I was older by several minutes, I used my older sister voice—which she ignored. She strode to the front door, and I followed, ready to stop her. When she pulled out her phone, I pretended not to listen.

"Tom, yes. Still here. Yes. Yes. No. What? Of course not. I'll be back by the afternoon. I totally understand, but you must realize somebody has to watch over Mother, and clearly, that's me."

"You?" I forgot I wasn't supposed to be eavesdropping. Babs dropped her phone in her purse and swung back around, glaring.

"Yes, me, because whenever *you're* in charge, something quite horrible always occurs. So maybe it's time I took over."

I pursed my lips, then bit back the grin just waiting in the wings. "All right, then, you take over." I got my things, then grabbed Dani before heading out the door and into the belly of the beast.

We all settled in—Pru and my mother up front, Matilda, Marcy, Hope, and Hilda at the little dinette area, and Rosa, Babs, Dani, and myself on the sectional.

"Girls, listen. We need to finalize the big day," Rosa said, beaming.

"By 'big day,' you mean the wedding, right?" I asked, just to be sure.

"*Sí, mis niñas.* We need to arrange a fitting for your dresses and finalize the arrangements. Dani, *tu papa* is coming, of course. We need escorts, and the more, the merrier."

Somehow, my brain couldn't put all that together, but then again, it wasn't my wedding. Thankfully. However, I did get a little dreamy eyed imagining how incredible a groom Devon would make. Then a maniacal shout from Hilda interrupted my musings.

"Brass tacky tarnation and holy hell, it's not the recipes they are after. It's the gold. Sean said that Steppenshitter fellow revealed the gold was one of Luckland's legendary secrets. Sean also said he'd been babbling about secret recipes. I bet those four were looking for the recipes for the gold."

"What do the recipes have to do with the legendary gold?" I asked.

"Nothing at all," Hope answered. "The La Pontes, Artemis, and Sylvester just thought they did. When Henri and Ginger got here, they realized the recipes *were* gold, so they copied them. Sylvester, though, he looked for something that would lead him to the gold, and he thought the recipes would do that, so he stole them."

That was a lot of conjecture, but it was just as plausible as any other hypothesis Devon and I had come up with.

"What about Artemis?" Dani asked.

"I bet he killed La Ponte because he thought Henri already knew where the gold was, but Henri wouldn't tell him, and Artemis killed him in a fit of rage," Prudence said. "The murder has everything to do with the gold and a group of over-aged lushes on spring break." That was quite a comment coming from the queen of over-aged lushes herself. Though admittedly, she'd toned it down since she reunited with Deputy Martin. I'd known them my whole life and, until recently, had no clue they were sweethearts. Tragic, really, that Prudence had to go through three truly terrifying Mr. Wrongs and an inordinate amount of booze to discover Martin had always been Mr. Right.

"Someone needs to translate for me. So, Henri was murdered because of gold that doesn't exist?" Dani asked quietly, smirking.

I shook my head because telling the ladies the gold didn't exist would likely start them off on another tangent. However, nobody said anything, which was odd because I was sure they'd eulogize the virtue of the gold and Founders' Day and what it meant to the town.

A little while later, we reached the outskirts of Luckland. Dani and I asked to be dropped off at the Manor as I was sure my cat and the goats needed attention. As the Luxmobile pulled up, Skye and Billy stood in the pasture, bleating away and hopping about like toddlers. 99 was framed in the window, casually napping and pretending she wasn't happy to see us. Then I spotted Devon sitting on the porch swing, leaning back, hands clasped behind his head, relaxed as could be. Simon leaned against one of the porch pillars, also quite relaxed. Neither of them seemed worried about the chaos that ruled the town.

Dani looked at me curiously. "Why do they look like they're *not* anxious to see us."

"I think it's a ruse. I think we're in for an earful," I muttered, squinting out the window to get a better look at Devon's face. "It's their fault for leaving us with the women. If they didn't want us involved in any of the ladies' schemes, they shouldn't have left us at the cabin."

"We're not involved in any scheme. The posse didn't even come up with a scheme," Dani said in protest.

I gestured at the two men on the porch. "They don't know that."

"Well, I am not obligated to listen to any lectures. I'm a free and independent woman who has no intention of getting off this bus." Dani laughed and twirled around, only to find Rosa right behind her shoving Dani's bag at her.

"Off you go, *mi hija*. We've got business to take care of," Rosa declared.

I grinned, grabbed Dani's elbow, and pulled her. "As if you'd ever let me face those two alone," I said. "We both know you wouldn't."

"Hmm, well. You might be right on that, but Simon has this way about him. It's unnerving," she murmured as we stepped out of the RV, then watched as it pulled away. We turned back toward the house. Simon and Devon were in the same spots, though now they wore some pretty serious smirks. Dani and I needed a game plan. I knew mine. I darted a glance at Dani, who appeared to brace herself. Then, nodding at each other, we walked toward the inevitable firing squad.

CHAPTER TWENTY-FIVE

"Well, girls, have you decided on your vows? The big day is Saturday, and we've not much time. Are you all going to take your vows at once or two at a time? Colin needs to know. Are you writing your own? Do you want Colin to read them?" Mom asked.

I sat back on my mom's patio chair and glanced at the ladies seated around the table.

It had been two weeks since Devon and Simon greeted our return from the cabin with a somewhat condescending diatribe on criminal investigations. I knew they thought we'd become involved with another of the ladies' schemes, and even though I had told the two lawmen there had been no plan other than wedding plans, they had still informed Dani and me that we were *not, under any circumstances,* to investigate crimes on our own. I was used to it, of course. Being Devon's partner didn't change his slightly old-fashioned but totally ridiculous notion that I needed his protection all the time. Dani, on the other hand, was simply not accustomed to any man telling her what to do. She was also a bit sensitive because of a recent encounter with Jonathan Steppenhoffer's son—another hypnotist who tried to get inside Dani's mind and flush out information about Luckland's gold.

So, instead of solving mysteries, we were busy with wedding plans. Triple wedding plans, which really weren't too complicated until you got deep into the weeds, like the vows, for example. A simple topic that turned into an afternoon fiasco.

"Marcy and I have each written our own vows," Hope said, answering one of my mom's questions.

"Oh. I thought you were going to quote something for both of us, Hope. I'm not sure I can write my own," Marcy said. She appeared panicked.

"Well, I just want whatever Colin comes up with, as long as it's speedy and appropriate," Prudence announced.

"Trey and I will be singing ours, naturally," Matilda said with a grin.

"So, two at a time, then," my mother muttered. She seemed taken aback. "Can't we keep this a little simpler?"

"You think because we're all getting married at the same time, we should have exactly the same vows?" asked Hope. "That's a bit unfair, don't you think?"

"Well, if you would have just learned to sing, this wouldn't be a problem," Matilda grumbled.

"Girls, please. It's all going to work out," Rosa said.

"I have an idea. Why don't you let me organize the ceremony to accommodate all your wishes." There, that should sort out that problem.

"Oh, and how will you do that?" My mother's voice held a hint of sarcasm.

"Mother, really. Pippa has photographed a ton of weddings. She has some experience in all this," Babs said, backing me up. I almost wanted to hug her. Almost.

"I'll make it happen. I promise." And I would. "Just have

your vows to me by tomorrow night. Email them over. Matilda, if you need music, then send me a soundtrack. Tell me what you need. I understand we'll be using a playlist Trey's musician buddies put together. This way, we can ensure we'll have what you want."

Babs frowned. "Wait, no live music?"

"You want the starring acts of Mullet Madness at the wedding?" I whispered in mock horror.

"No, I was thinking a nice little quartet. Like at my wedding," Babs replied.

I looked pointedly at each woman around the table, then at Babs.

She pursed her lips, then laughed. "Never mind."

"Very well then, let's move on," my mother said. "The rehearsal dinner is Friday night. That's only two days from now. Babs, have you arranged everything?"

"Check. My house, seven sharp."

"Very good. Pippa, do you have what you need for the wedding photos?"

"Check." I was well prepared. I'd even ordered a new timer for the shots that would include me.

My mom smiled. "Well, that just leaves the bachelorette party."

Dani and I looked at each other and sighed.

"Mom, do you really think that's a good idea? We discussed this, remember? You ladies have a terrible track record with this kind of thing." I didn't want to sound negative, but they had a very, very bad track record.

"Oh, pishposh," Hilda said as she stepped on the patio to join us. "Sorry I'm late, girls, but there was a last-minute snafu in the pole dancing lineup."

"Did you really just say that?" I looked at Hilda as she squeezed in on the bench seat next to Rosa.

"What? Snafu?" Hilda laughed. "Seriously, there's a fabulous little dancing duo out of Denver that does multi-sexual events." She stared at all of us, then burst out laughing. "Oh, my stars, you are all so gullible. After the rehearsal dinner, we'll have a lovely wine and dessert affair. At my place."

"Hilda, what do you mean by *your place*?" Marcy looked shell-shocked while the rest of us watched the interaction.

"Well, you don't think I can stay at the Inn forever, do you? I found a wonderful little place. It's a sweet little cottage just at the edge of town. The little gray one with burgundy trim."

"Oh my god, that's my old place!" I'd recently learned the Luckland Ladies Trust, which consisted of my mother and her besties, owned the cottage. "So, are you renting the place?"

"Oh no, I need to put down roots, and real estate here is hard to come by, so I bought it outright."

That was when Marcy looked at Hope, who leaned back and winced. Then Marcy continued to throw death glares at the other women.

"You all sold Hilda a house. Here. In Luckland?" Marcy was clearly not happy. At that point, she was mad as a hatter. Or madder.

"Can we get back to the plans, please?" my mother asked, her voice calm as if Hilda hadn't just dropped an atomic bomb. "There's one final detail that's perhaps a bit delicate but necessary to bring up."

"Well, bring it on up, sugar," Hilda said. "The clock is ticking."

My mom gave Hilda a sidelong look, but Hilda was too tough for even her. "Fine, the seating at the wedding will be tricky. Are we using bride's side, groom's side, or at-large seating?"

"Mom, nobody cares where anyone sits," I said.

"Of course they do. They just pretend they don't." Babs was

suddenly the authority on etiquette. "Since there are three couples, we'll simply have three sections. One for each couple."

I smiled. "That's a fabulous idea, Babs."

"Did you doubt I could have one?"

"And that was quite snarky. You impress me, dear sister." I grinned, threw my arm about her shoulder, and squeezed. That ought to muss up her hair and get her riled.

Strangely, it didn't. She grinned back. Perhaps being around me more brought out her inner child. I couldn't wait to see what else Babs had hidden inside.

"Good news, ladies." Simon seemed quite chipper as he and Devon came out to the patio, taking us all by surprise if anyone's expression was anything to go by.

"Hello, boys. What do you have for us?" Matilda asked.

"We've identified Sylvester the Cat," Simon said. "The prints we took from his room matched those on IAFIS, the FBI's fingerprint database."

"Who is he?" Prudence asked. "The reverend from Palm Beach, like we suspected?"

"Exactly. The reverend, AKA Sylvester, was nothing but a two-bit grifter who spent a few years in prison after running a traveling revival show," Devon said. "He also has a few thousand followers on TikTok and believed staging a dead polar bear would distract everyone so he could burglarize the office, only he didn't have time. So, he tried again."

"So, Sylvester is the culinary slasher," Hilda declared, not mincing words. "Are you going to arrest him?"

"He *has* been arrested, but not for killing the chef. When questioned about the recipes, which the police found at his premises, he said he thought they would lead him to gold."

"Ha, I knew it," Hilda exclaimed. "It was about the gold!"

"That means Henri didn't hire him to steal the recipes," I said. "We got that wrong."

"It was a good theory though," Simon replied.

"There's more," Devon said with a grin. He did enjoy it when cases wrapped up. "Artemis Ainsley and Ginger La Ponte have been implicated in Henri La Ponte's murder, and the Taos police have them in custody."

"That's not too much of a surprise," I said. "What gave them away?"

"Their affair and the fact they knew he had allergies that could kill him. The police are still questioning them to find out why they tried to point the finger at Hilda for Henri's murder, but there's something else we need to tell you." Simon glanced at Devon, who grinned.

"We found four of your shoeboxes."

"Ginger had the shoeboxes?" My mother sounded stunned. "Did she open them?"

"Well, the Taos police found four shoeboxes in her possession. Right now, they're in evidence, and at this stage, I don't know whether she opened them or not."

"Devon, you must get those back immediately." Matilda stood and squared her shoulders as she stared at her son, daring him to defy her.

"You'll get them back, I promise. Just not yet."

Her frustration seemed to infuse the posse. They all looked about ready to protest or string him up by the neck, so I thought it best to diffuse the situation.

"How did she get the boxes? We have a video of the Panellos carrying them off from the yard sale," I said.

Simon cleared his throat—probably aware of how close he was to a lynch mob. "According to my source, Ginger and Henri were walking around town when a pair of men just handed the boxes off to them. Ginger said they told Henri and herself to have at it."

"These Panellos, they were the guys that held you all at

gunpoint?" Hilda looked around for confirmation. "They bought the boxes then just gave them to a perfect stranger who ended up murdering her husband who had used the café's recipes for his own gain? Is this some sort of reality show script?"

"Hilda, reality shows don't have scripts," Hope said.

"Of course they do. They're just unwritten."

That gave us all pause.

"Look, everyone, settle down. The criminals are behind bars. Well, some of them. So now we can all relax and have a perfect wedding weekend," Babs declared.

Somehow, I didn't think so. Another hunch. Something wasn't right in Luckland.

CHAPTER TWENTY-SIX

On Christmas Eve, Devon and I enjoyed some much-needed quiet time in front of our miraculously fully operational fireplace. Snuggled up on the couch and sharing a throw blanket, nothing could ruin our romantic moment—except the pounding on the door.

After a quick rock, paper, scissors, I answered it. "Dani, what's wrong? I thought you were with your mom at the Inn."

"Papa."

I gave her a hug and ushered her in. "What about him?"

"He's here and giving Simon the third degree."

I grinned. "Uh-oh. Did you tell your dad nothing's going on?" I wondered if Dani truly realized there was definitely and obviously something going on.

"I did, and he had the nerve to scoff at me."

"Dani, anyone can see you and Simon have a thing," Devon remarked. I sat next to him, and he ran his fingers along my shoulders, reminding me of *our* thing.

Dani sank onto the little rug in front of the fire and pulled 99 onto her lap, making herself quite at home. "Nothing has happened. I repeat, nothing."

"Yet," I said. "It will. Your dad is just surveying the landscape, getting a feel for what's happening. He hardly ever interferes, you know that."

"He's going to scare him off," Dani muttered.

Devon smiled. "So, that's what this is about. No worries. Simon doesn't scare easily. You didn't see me run when Colin interrogated me."

"Wait? My dad? He would never." Not once had my dad ever interfered in my life.

"He said if I hurt you, I would pay. Said he'd whoop the… crap out of me." Devon laughed and rolled his eyes. "As if."

"Oh, he could have, wonder boy, don't doubt that," I replied with a smirk. My dad might be soft and cuddly, but he was fierce when it came to his family.

Dani smiled, but then sighed. Her sitting there moping wasn't helping her any. "Dani, it's Christmas Eve. Now get yourself back over there and spend time with your folks. I'm sure they're done having *the talk*, as it were, and it's safe."

Dani rolled her eyes at me but stood and placed 99 on my lap. After she grabbed her coat, hat, and scarf, she turned back to me and grinned. "Don't do anything I wouldn't do." She laughed as she strode out with a wave of her hand.

"Oh, please," Devon said with a shake of his head. "There's not much that girl won't do."

"Devon!" I laughed and elbowed him.

"What say we go try, eh?" Devon winked and stood before he grabbed my hand and pulled me up alongside him.

"Bad news, Pip," Devon said as I entered the kitchen the next morning. It was the big day. The day of the triple wedding. The day of all days. Christmas Day.

"And Merry Christmas to you too," I whispered, leaning up to give him a kiss or two. "You're referring to that lovely billowing fluff out there called snow, aren't you?"

It was a sight to behold: a beautiful white Christmas—which would have been ideal if we didn't have a wedding to pull off. From the looks of things, with snow falling at an inch an hour, the roads would be treacherous, and having the ceremony at the outdoor gazebo wasn't going to happen. We'd have to move it indoors. It would only be a matter of minutes before my phone exploded with messages, so I took the steaming mug of life-giving nectar Devon offered me, and we sat down to contemplate the latest Luckland disaster.

"I seem to recall mentioning the possibility of snow, Pip," Devon said, oblivious to the fact I recognized an *I told you so* when I heard one.

"Neither here nor there. Now, we need a plan B."

"Which is?"

"B is for Babs," I responded as I grabbed my phone and began furiously texting her.

Me: Please tell me you have an idea.

Babs: Meet you at the Inn.

Me: Just me?

Babs: No, bring the muscle too.

Devon and I arrived in one piece, though driving even a short distance in a white-out was brutally terrifying. Perhaps not as terrifying as what we found at the Inn, which was Hilda directing traffic in the lobby. By traffic, I meant an entire cast of characters moving everything from chairs and tables to what appeared to be statues of Cupids, though I would swear one was a statue of David. What appeared to be satin sheets covered the unfinished floors and the drywall. Twinkling lights that had hung on the gazebo last night now hung around the lobby to direct a gaze from anything unsightly—like the barrel of sawdust in the corner.

Oddly, Hilda had ditched her cane and seemed to be moving about with amazing ease. Maybe it was a Christmas sort of miracle. Or maybe the cane had just been a prop all along. Babs stood in the middle of it all, her head turning as if watching a chaotic ping-pong tournament. I knew this was not going to end well, so I did what my gut told me and let out a shrieking whistle. When everyone stopped, I looked at Devon in hopes he would use his authoritative tone to encourage coop- eration.

"If you could please give Babs your attention, it would be appreciated," he said.

Babs threw him a grateful smile, then looked at me and nodded in the direction of the kitchen. I assumed that meant she wanted me to check on whatever was going on in there and to leave the lobby lunacy to her.

The kitchen seemed under control. In fact, Chef Harris appeared quite efficient. Watching him dart back and forth from the pantry, the cold storage, and the freezer, he had a certain grace. Like a choreographed dance. Probably due to the music I assumed played through his earbuds. I couldn't tell from his movements what he was listening to. From my wedding gigs, I knew people had certain moves based on the music. There was the jazzy sway, the tapping fingers of pop, and the pounding feet of rock. Usually, it was easy to tell, but as I watched Monte, I couldn't figure it out. I waited for a moment, then plunged in.

"Say, Chef." I looked directly at him and pointed to his ear, indicating he should remove his earbud for a second.

"What's up, Pippa?"

"Just wondering what you're listening to. You know, while you cook."

"Oh, nothing fascinating, different podcasts, audiobooks, those kinds of things. Right now, it's a mystery. Murder at the Pier."

I smiled. "Oh, that's TK's new one. I'm reading that now, so no spoilers," I said in warning. "Well, carry on. I'm off to check on the flowers." Making sure the flowers were exactly where they were meant to be was on my original list of things to do, so though our venue had changed, I still had to follow through. Then I could relax, at least until this crazy ceremony got started.

I had to hand it to Babs. She'd done an amazing job organizing the lobby's transformation from haunted house to a winter garden wonderland. From my vantage point on the balcony, I looked down to the far end where a hastily constructed yet beautiful satin chuppah stood. Hilda had insisted Marcy marry under the Jewish ceremonial canopy, and since we couldn't be outdoors under the stars as Ashkenazi tradition required, Hilda had made sure there were about a thousand twinkling lights along the edges of the canopy. The white, high-back wedding chairs, neatly rowed into three sections, one for each of the brides' guests, had tiny bells attached to ribbons of lace affixed to the back as a nod to their Irish heritage.

The mahogany rails of the wide, grand staircase leading to the mezzanine balcony gleamed while stunning bouquets of deep red poppies intertwined with the flowing ribbon of champagne fabric woven through the rails. My mom had told me the women would use the upstairs rooms as dressing rooms, so the stairs provided the perfect grand entrance for everyone.

Unfortunately, Trey's band members, who Trey wanted to

play live at the wedding, hadn't made it because of the blizzard, but Babs had somehow managed to find a string quartet. Technically, the quartet was the high school music teacher and three of her best students. However, as perfect as the scene in front of me was, a clear sense of foreboding overtook me. I only hoped it didn't mean I'd be the one to ruin the ceremony by tripping and tumbling down the stairs face-first. Then I worried one of the betrothed would back out, the power would go out, or the ceiling would cave in. Before I could contemplate any further catastrophe, I turned to head to the room Dani and I had grabbed to get changed in—and came face to face with a woman wearing a red dress.

I didn't recognize her and assumed she was Martin or Trey's guest. "Are you looking for something or someone?" I asked.

At the tip of her head, I realized two things at once. First, she was slightly transparent, and second, her red dress hadn't been originally red. I gasped and took a step back. She took one forward and held out her hand. In it, balanced on her palm, sat a gold nugget.

"Hey."

I almost screamed but recognized Devon's voice a split second before he slipped a strong and comfortable arm around my waist.

"Settle down, Red, it's all good," Devon said as he held me tight. He wasn't talking about the apparition that stood in front of me.

"You can't see her, can you?" I carefully pointed to the woman who still held out the gold nugget to me.

"See who?"

I glanced up at him. "The Scarlet Lady." I instantly knew why everyone called her that and what colored her dress. Someone had murdered her for that nugget or the information about its location. I shuddered, and she blinked out of existence.

I turned into Devon's chest and hugged him. "She's gone."

"Are you—"

"I'm fine." I took a deep breath, then looked up at him. "How'd you know there was something wrong?"

"Your body language." He kissed the top of my head. "Are you sure you're all right?"

I nodded, then offered him a trembling smile, though I couldn't help but wonder why she'd shown herself to me today. Was it a warning? Was she trying to tell me something?

He squeezed me tight. "Don't worry. Everything is going to be fine."

"I hope so," I whispered. "I hope so."

CHAPTER TWENTY-SEVEN

The rich sounds of the string quartet floated up the stairway with the introductory notes to the ever-popular wedding processional, Pachelbel's Canon. Its slow, graceful melody had all of us taking a deep breath as we readied ourselves.

Escorted by Babs and Tom, Leah began the procession, holding a basket of flower petals and stopping on every step to toss one petal in the air. I figured if she only tossed one on each step, it would take a half hour to get to the bottom. Pedro escorted Dani and me, and we started our descent after Leah had gone about halfway down. Behind us, my mom and dad brought up the rear, and we all took our places to the side of the chuppah and watched as Matilda and Prudence made their entrance, each with an arm looped through Devon's, who looked incredibly handsome in his rental tux. Once they reached the bottom, Hope and Marcy made their descent, accompanied by Simon—also a handsome devil in a tux.

The women glowed in their elegant, simple satin gowns. Dani and I wore similar gowns, except in a deep green, while Babs was in red. Very in keeping with the holiday.

Colin waited under the chuppah with Trey and Martin, who

each went to escort their brides as they approached. When all three couples were in place, the ceremony began.

"Welcome all. On this glorious Christmas Day, we are gathered to celebrate the marriages of Trey Marks and Matilda McDonald, Prudence Smalley and Martin O'Hara, and of course, Hope Santella and Marcy Feingold. Each of the couples has prepared their own vows, and we'll go ahead and let them speak those now. If anyone in this room has any objection to any of these couples tying the knot, well…" My dad coughed lightly. "I suggest you get the hell out."

A wave of laughter spread throughout the room, putting everyone at ease, except Lois Thorpe, who appeared tense. Maybe she had an objection. That was interesting.

Nobody knew what to expect as Matilda and Trey stepped forward. All decorum went out the window when those two were together. The big question had been what song they would choose.

Turned out they fooled us all. They didn't sing. They turned to face each other, and Matilda placed one hand on Trey's cheek.

"Trey, now I've found you, I'm never letting go." There was a vulnerability in Matilda just then. She was no longer my *Aunt Tillie* at that moment.

Trey placed his hand on Matilda's cheek. "I'm counting on it, Tillie. It's you and me now. Well, you, me, and our son."

I watched as they gazed at each other, each silently acknowledging their own past transgressions, the hope in their eyes unmistakable. They turned to face my dad, then stepped back, allowing Prudence and Martin to step forward, who turned to each other and clasped each other's hands.

"I'm sorry." Prudence's voice was barely a whisper.

"Me too," Martin whispered back.

"You are the only one I've ever loved," Prudence said softly. "Only you."

"Ditto," Martin said with a smile that lit up his face. "Only you."

Prudence and Martin, high school sweethearts, were finally getting their happily ever after.

Stepping back, still holding hands, they made room for Hope and Marcy to move forward under the chuppah.

"The first time we met, I knew you were the one," Marcy said. "I knew we belonged together. It just took a while for the world to catch up." She smiled down at Hope...and waited.

"I know you thought I'd come up with the cleverest of vows, Marce, but I find myself at a loss for words. You mean every-thing to me. You always have. I'm just so glad we can finally say, 'I do.' I never thought this day would come."

There wasn't a dry eye in the place. Except maybe Lois. What a grumpy old woman. Hilda gave her the death stare.

"If you'd all take each other's hands and repeat after me. And listen carefully." My dad emphasized that last bit as he looked at Prudence. She had a knack for not paying attention.

As my dad began his little sermon, which I thought he copied off the internet, he said something about when life puts an obstacle in your way, you go around it. I suddenly had a vision of Monte and his audiobooks. With sudden and absolute clarity, I realized what that meant. Because Monte had dyslexia, he didn't read books. Instead, he listened. The significance of that threw a lightning bolt through me. However, there was nothing I could do because I had to wait for the ceremony to end. Finally, when each couple broke the traditional glass, and the whoops and hollers began, I rushed over to Devon, grabbed his hand, and pulled hard so he'd follow me to the rear hallway.

"This better be earth-shattering. My mother just got

married. I should be hugging her, not sneaking off with you," he said with a smirk.

"No time for that, lover boy. Monte. Monte was in the kitchen listening to an audiobook earlier. Murder at the Pier. Which means..." I looked at Devon in horror.

"Which means he also listened to Murder at the Chateau," Devon said.

When a click sounded behind us, we froze.

"You two start walking. To the kitchen. Don't make a sound. Don't reach for anything," Monte said, his voice a menacing whisper.

I swallowed and took a breath, then moved alongside Devon toward the swinging doors at the end of the hall leading to the kitchen. I swore Monte's breath ghosted the back of my neck, though I was also positive he wasn't that close behind us. Perhaps the breath belonged to the more ethereal kind.

Reaching the doors, I said a quick prayer to the powers that be that none of the catering staff were in the kitchen. I didn't want anyone else in danger.

CHAPTER TWENTY-EIGHT

"Hɪ-ʏᴀʜ!"

I flinched at the scream, assuming Monte was going a little nutty after he'd forced me at gunpoint to tie Devon's hands behind his back. Monte had then tied my hands and shoved Devon and me into a kitchen chair. I'd hoped Devon could free himself as I'd made sure to tie his hands loosely.

The crashing sound and loud thump that followed the scream were even more jarring. Devon and I twisted slightly to find none other than Hilda, arms raised and holding a large cast iron skillet. Monte lay crumpled on the floor, the gun just inches from Devon's leg. He quickly kicked the gun away in case Monte wasn't entirely out, though, from my vantage point, he clearly was. How a ninety-year-old woman could knock out a man as large as Monte was astonishing. I was speechless.

Devon wasn't.

"Hilda, that was well done."

"They didn't call me headbanger for nothing, you know," she replied with a laugh.

"Do I want to know?" I asked, letting out a sigh of relief mixed with a massive amount of pent-up fear.

"You certainly do not. Now, your partner should be here to untie you any minute, so if you'll excuse me, Finn promised me a dance."

Devon and I looked at each other, stunned that she'd left us there.

"Did she really just..." we said in unison.

Moments later, Simon came barreling through the doors, swinging them so hard they cracked against the counters. Then I heard sirens. I could hear everyone shouting and running around, trying to see what was amiss. I assumed the deputies would come in through the back. Devon leaned over, gave me a quick kiss, and twisted around so Simon could cut the rope.

"Ever hear of ladies first?" I narrowed my eyes at Devon, then shot the same look at Simon as he busily freed Devon.

"Freeing you is *my* job, Pip, and mine alone." Devon grabbed the shears Simon had used and quickly cut me loose. After pulling me up with both hands, Devon wrapped his arms tightly around me, squeezing me just enough to let me know I mattered and asking my forgiveness. The uniformed officers charging in, followed quickly by some suits, probably feds, and several locals all trying to get in on the action, shattered our momentary solitude. I slipped out of Devon's arms and slid past them all to see what was going on in the real world. Well, in Luckland's version, anyway. Spotting Dani with her parents, I hurried over and tried to remain composed as I yanked her away with me.

"This is a disaster."

"It's Monte, then?" Dani asked, though it seemed a little rhetorical.

"Of course it's Monte." I nodded toward the kitchen. "Hopefully, they'll get him out of there quickly, so at least we can feed the guests and keep them occupied."

"We've got it covered," Hope said as she floated by with Marcy.

"No, it's your wedding, Hope. We've got this," Rosa said as she raced to beat them to the kitchen.

"Nobody can go in there yet, so you all need to stop right there." Simon's voice seemed to come out of the blue. The lobby wasn't all that big, and when close to one hundred people milled about in confusion, chaos was not far behind.

Trey and Matilda stood behind the Inn's registration desk, deep in conversation. Suddenly, the cheerful bopper sounds of eighties music filled the space. Hilda and Finn immediately got in the center of it all, replaying the final dance scene from Dirty Dancing. Hilda ran down the aisle into Finn's arms, who swept her high into the air. I hoped an ambulance was standing by.

Dani and I were dumbstruck, though not at the idea of Hilda attempting such a daring move. We were dumbstruck because she and Finn pulled it off. Cheers erupted from the guests, drowning out the commotion going on in the back. Perhaps there was a method to Hilda's madness after all.

Once we'd all settled down and something tamer began to play, I spun at a familiar whisper in my ear.

"Our turn?"

I couldn't resist. Dancing with Devon in a tux and me in a gown was one of those fairy-tale moments I denied ever wanting but secretly always wished for. I wrapped my arms around his neck and took a moment just to breathe him in. Devon had a way of calming my senses, and I waited until I was completely relaxed before quizzing him.

"You knew, didn't you?"

"I suspected."

"You could have clued me in, Devon. I was alone in that kitchen with him, you know. Anything could have happened."

"But it didn't. I'd never let anything happen to you. You

know that." He smiled down at me and kissed the tip of my nose. "How about we sneak off after all this wraps up?"

I was just about to agree when the ringing tone of someone tapping a glass filled the air. We turned. My mother held her glass in one hand and a spoon in the other.

"Time for the official first dance. If we can have all our couples on the floor?"

The guests formed a circle, allowing room for the three couples to dance. Devon stood behind me, his arms wrapped around my waist. I leaned my head on his chest. Beside us, Dani stood next to Simon, who'd casually placed his hand on the small of her back. It was a quiet gesture that spoke volumes.

Matilda, Hope, Marcy, and Prudence floated into the center of the dance floor, Trey and Martin right behind them. When the intro to a classic Marvin Gaye song began, everyone smiled. It was inevitable people would quietly sing along, though the soft crooning coming out of Devon was entirely unexpected. He rarely sang—at least in my presence.

I looked up, catching his gaze, and even without the words or the ceremony, I knew we were as tied together as the couples who had just said their vows. It wasn't until Dani nudged me that I realized the song had ended. Devon realized it too, and we laughed, still wrapped up in each other.

Simon and Devon didn't stick around long. They had to head off and deal with Monte. Eventually, they returned, only to let us know the FBI would be interviewing us.

"Interrogate, you mean," I said.

"No, Pip, the word is interview. Monte tied you up and held you at gunpoint, which requires the FBI to debrief you so they can file appropriate charges. Hilda needs to explain herself as well. Clearly, she was saving us, but she has to tell her story."

"Okay, and what about you? I do recall you sitting right beside me, also tied up." I still didn't understand how police procedures worked. No matter how involved Devon and Simon were in any situation, they were treated differently.

"I'll have my turn, I promise."

"Can I ask how the police and FBI got here so quickly?" Though I knew Simon was an FBI agent, I didn't understand how agents from Denver got to Luckland within minutes of Monte taking Devon and me hostage.

Devon hugged me. "I'll tell you later."

As the last of the guests slowly made their way out of the Inn, the newlyweds, along with the rest of the wedding party, gathered around one of the larger tables. There was a clear sense of post-party exhaustion. Down at one end of the table, Matilda and Trey sat in one of the "couple chairs" so designated because it was literally big enough for two—a rattan papasan chair with big fluffy white cushions. I wished I had snagged it for Devon and me. To their right, Prudence and Martin sat in high-back chairs pulled close to each other, holding hands, Pru's head on Martin's shoulder. Opposite them sat Marcy and Hope. They'd pulled up a bench seat, and Hope sat lengthwise, feet on Marcy's lap. I realized I'd been derelict in my duties, and with a pat on Devon's shoulder, I got up, retrieved my camera from behind the reservation desk, and began photographing the afterparty. It was almost, photographically, a better way to capture moments. This was real life. Wedding ceremonies generally produced beautiful photos, but tension often filled them. The shots I got of everyone unwinding were truly wonderful. They would be the highlight of the wedding album.

The champagne still flowed freely, so I paused for a refill. Sitting down on Devon's lap, I leaned back and closed my eyes for just a moment. Then the voices around me all seemed to quiet down abruptly. I opened one eye, curious, and spotted Simon standing at the other end of the table behind Dani's chair. He had a certain look about him that he got when he was about to solve a case. Though I knew this one was already solved, I was still all ears.

"You're all dying to know, aren't you?" He looked from one to the other at the table.

"Was it really Monte who killed the chef?" Hilda asked from her position on the throne chair.

"I think it was Ginger," Hope said, her tone emphatic.

"No. The crazy puppeteer did it. He killed the chef. Monte is quite innocent." Prudence lifted her glass in a toast, called out "bottom's up," and downed the contents.

"Don't be silly. The man held Devon and Pippa at gunpoint. So, we all know Monte is the murderer, but there's a lot we don't know. I think we need more information," Matilda said. "Tell us something we don't know."

Simon nodded. "All right then, but I need to go back to the beginning. We know Henri and Ginger came to Luckland to seek recipes, gold, or both. The Panellos handed them four shoeboxes and—"

"Where are they?"

"When can we have them back?"

"*Did* she open them?"

"Ladies! Please!" Simon gave each of them a pointed look. "To answer your questions, the boxes are still being processed, I'm not sure when you can have them back, and yes, she did open them but said she wasn't interested in their contents."

The women all gasped, and I worried at how pale they'd gone. Hilda frowned, and Devon and Simon glanced at each other. Dani and Babs didn't seem to understand the significance for a moment until Dani's eyes widened.

"She's the one who threatened the posse."

CHAPTER TWENTY-NINE

Simon shook his head. "She says not, and from her reaction to her interrogation, and she *was* interrogated and not just questioned, Devon and I believe her."

"Actually, we don't think either Ginger or Henri had anything to do with the threats the ladies received," Devon said.

I turned to look up at him, not liking his answer. If neither Ginger nor Henri threatened the ladies, then it was someone who had one of the other two boxes. That was not good news.

"What about the cheesecake and lasagna recipes they leaked? Why would they do that?" I asked.

"According to Ginger, Henri leaked the recipes because he was jealous of the café's success. With the recipes online, he hoped the café would lose its customers and go out of business," Simon commented.

"Well, he failed there because business was so good, we had to move to bigger premises," Hope said, a trifle smug.

"Criminals. Most of them are not the sharpest tool in the shed," my mom said.

Simon smiled. "We also know Ginger asked Artemis to help

her find the gold, so once they had it, they could be rid of Henri once and for all. When Henri died, Ginger thought Artemis did it. He thought she did. He didn't think anyone would realize he mimicked Henri and Hilda on that tape and honestly thought she'd be a suspect."

"So, Ginger and Artemis tried to frame Hilda to protect the other, but what made them think either attempt would stick?" Marcy asked.

"They knew Hilda is TK Moreaux, courtesy of Sean at Royal Palm Pavilions, so they each believed they could set her up, something to do with her being a murder mystery writer and in Taos at the same time someone murdered Henri. We know Artemis saw her at the RV park, but so did Ginger. She was hiding in his camper. When questioned, they also tried to convince the authorities that she'd based Murder at the Chateau on a previous attempt to murder Henri at Royal Palm."

"I did no such thing! I never even met the man," Hilda declared.

"Sean confirmed that for us, Hilda," Devon said.

I suddenly remembered Devon had said Ginger had leveled other "odd" accusations against Hilda, and I assumed that was what he meant.

"When did you get all this information?" I asked. Surely Devon and Simon hadn't received it today.

"Actually, I received an emailed report last night," Simon said. "I haven't had a chance to talk to any of you, what with today's celebrations."

"But you had time to tell Devon," I murmured, giving Devon a baleful glare for not clueing me in earlier. That was why he suspected Monte—because he no longer suspected Ginger and Artemis.

Simon inclined his head. "Yes, but while you were all getting beautiful."

Well, that mollified me a little.

"So, that brings us back to Monte," Simon said.

"I just don't see why he'd murder La Ponte," Marcy stated sadly. "Monte was so nice and so talented."

I turned to her. "While he had Devon and me tied up in the kitchen, Monte tried to explain what had happened. He said he had been having a hard time getting La Ponte to allow him to add his own recipes to the restaurant menu. Monte was getting more and more frustrated. Henri had been winning awards and gaining fame with his recipes. Sorry, Hilda's, Marcy's, and Hope's recipes. Anyway, Henri refused to 'taint' his menu with second-rate dishes even though Monte was allowed to serve wedding parties. Then Monte overheard Henri and Ginger discussing the recipes. Henri said he needed to go back to Luckland to get some new ones from 'those hapless women' and realized they weren't Henri's recipes at all. Monte said he confronted Henri and told him he knew Henri was a fake. Henri threatened to fire him."

"So, La Ponte's death was premeditated," my dad said.

Devon shook his head. "That's something we have to find out for sure, but Monte claims La Ponte's death was an accident. He said when the chef reached for a custom spice blend Monte had created that contained sumac, which La Ponte was known to be allergic to, Monte was angry and didn't say anything. Monte's defense is that he didn't know the sumac would kill Henri, only that it would make him sick. Also, Monte said that as he didn't give the sumac to Henri but simply didn't stop him from tasting the spice blend, it wasn't his fault La Ponte died."

Prudence snorted. "You don't buy that do you? Trust me. It's not that easy to off someone."

The room grew silent as everyone stared at Pru.

"What? I watch crime shows too, you know. Plus, if La Ponte

had allergies like that, he'd have had an EpiPen nearby. Why couldn't Henri or Monte get to it on time?"

"Actually, I asked Monte that, and he said he couldn't find it," Devon said.

"Maybe Ginger had hidden it," Marcy stated.

I believed she still hoped Monte was innocent, but it seemed likely Monte had listened to Hilda's Murder at the Chateau, and that was where he'd gotten the idea of how to kill La Ponte.

"Best we leave it for the DA to sort out," Devon said.

"Fair enough, but can we get back to the boxes?" Prudence was on a roll. "We need to get them back."

There was something in Prudence's tone that set me on edge. "I understand losing them was upsetting for you, but there's been an awful lot of interest in Luckland's gold since they went missing. Is there something in those boxes that has something to do with the legend?"

All six women, including Rosa and Marcy, seemed to find their nails interesting. I was fed up with their aversion to revealing their secrets. "Ladies?"

After a moment, when each woman had some sort of silent communication, my mom stood. "The contents have to do with the sacred ground Luckland is built on, and about the spirits that will rise if the ground is disturbed, which is why we need to get them back as soon as possible."

I searched my mom's face. "You mean to say that all this time, we've been searching for boxes that contain a story to a legend that isn't real?"

My mom frowned. "All legends have a basis of truth, Pippa."

The ladies all looked resolute. They were not going to budge on their beliefs, and I couldn't really refute them. I'd seen first-hand Luckland's spirits roaming around town. I shuddered again as I remembered the Scarlet Lady.

"Okay, so what are you saying?"

"That's as much as we are willing or able to tell you, but with only four boxes recovered, you still need to find the other two," Matilda said.

Prudence nodded. "Because whoever has them still has access to vital information that could harm Luckland."

Harm Luckland? I glanced at Devon, but he seemed just as confused as me.

"Yes. And according to Lali, whoever has them is someone local," Matilda remarked.

I wasn't sure I heard that right. "Lali? You asked her about the shoeboxes?"

My mom sniffed. "Of course. We wouldn't waste such an opportunity."

Devon sighed. "And she told you the other two boxes are in Luckland?"

Hope took Marcy's hand. "Well, it makes sense. Only a resident would know the importance of those boxes."

All had been relatively quiet in Luckland for the last six months if I didn't count random ghostly sightings and the odd "gold hunter." At least nothing had sent Devon and me scurrying across the country with the ladies, trying to keep them out of mischief.

Instead, the ladies kept busy with their spouses, and Devon and I spent our time finishing the renovations on Mystic Manor before the next disaster happened—because it definitely would.

Then, on opening night of Murphy's Playhouse, our new community theater, we sat cozied up together, excited about the show and sneaking an award-worthy kiss as the lights went down. We were having a moment—until a tingle ran down my spine, and my phone buzzed.

Babs: Emergency with Mother. Come quick!

SNEAK PEEK AT THE NEXT LUCKLAND MYSTERY
VENGEFUL SPIRITS AND A LOST GOLD MINE

CHAPTER ONE

I shook my head because, seriously, couldn't Babs, my intrepid twin sister, get our mother to the theater on time without it being a major catastrophe? My mom should already be standing at the front doors, two of her BFFs all set to lead her down the aisle. So, I had no idea what could have gone wrong. My best guess; our dear mother refused to wear a blindfold because she didn't particularly like surprises any more than I did. Either that or she thought the blindfold would ruin her blonde bob.

With a sigh, I rose to my feet. Then my phone buzzed again.

Babs: All's fine.

I sat back down.

"What is it?" Dani, my BFF, whispered beside me.

"Babs and her theatrics."

Dani grinned. "She gets it from your mom."

I chuckled just as an expectant hush took over the crowd seated in the rows and rows of red velvet upholstered chairs.

The audience was still, and everyone held their breath as my mom, blindfolded, gripped Hope's hand on one side and

Prudence's on the other and slowly walked toward the stage. Anticipation grew as she got closer. She had no clue what was happening—which was amazing because the entire town of Luckland was in on the surprise.

A few murmurs whispered throughout the theater as we waited for someone to lift the stage curtains and for Hope or Prudence to remove Mom's blindfold. Matilda, another of my mom's closest friends, stood just to the right of the stage, cueing someone on the other side to pull up the curtain.

Nothing happened. I glanced at Devon, my significant other, who sat on my other side from Dani. He narrowed his eyes.

Matilda lifted her arm and nodded once again. Still nothing. She frowned, then peeked around the curtain before she headed across the stage behind the long drapes. I guessed some poor teenager was about to get an earful. What I didn't expect was a blood-curdling scream.

Devon, Chief Marks when in uniform, jumped over the seats in front then hopped up on the stage, running off to the side where Matilda had screamed. Simon, his FBI buddy, was right behind him. My mother ripped off the blindfold and simply stared around in stunned silence. Martin O'Hara, local deputy sheriff and Prudence's husband, followed Devon and Simon to the back of the stage, and while other patrons stood and inched forward, I headed to my mom.

"What's happening?" she asked.

"Right now, I don't know, but I'm sure Devon can handle it," I said.

"That was Matilda's scream. Is she all right." Mom took a few steps toward the stage while Hope and Prudence appeared as confused as everyone else.

"This wasn't part of the show, I take it?" Dani asked as she came over.

"Of course not," Hope said, her brow furrowed.

"Ladies, gentlemen."

We all turned as Martin spoke from the stage.

"If you can all return to your seats for a moment. I'm afraid we'll have to cancel the show, and I'll need everyone here to give me their name as they leave." He descended the stage and strode to the front door, the previous murmurs now full cries of bewilderment.

I had no idea what they'd found backstage, but it spelled disaster.

It took half an hour, but eventually, everyone left. The only ones who remained inside were Devon, Simon, Martin, and the infamous Luckland Ladies, or the posse as I affectionally called my mother and her lifelong best friends.

I paused outside the front of the theater and took a breath. Thankfully, the night was clear, and the temperature wasn't too bad for June in Colorado. The gentle breeze was just cool enough to make the sweater I brought practical and not overkill.

I sighed. "Why is it nothing ever goes as planned in Luckland?"

Dani laughed beside me. "Because it's Luckland."

"Did you see what happened in there?" I asked her.

"No clue. Simon pushed me out the exit door before I could ask Matilda."

"Well damn. Guess we'll have to start texting."

I pulled up the Luckland Ladies group contact on my phone and fired away.

Me: What's going on?

We waited. Radio silence.

Me: Fine, we're coming back in.

I muttered as I typed. I must have muttered a bit too loud.

"No, Pip, you're not." Devon's voice sounded firm from behind my right ear.

I turned my head and looked up. "What happened? Why did Matilda scream? There aren't any bodies, are there?" I was really only kidding, but the look on his face was not filled with humor.

"Oh my god, there's a body?" Dani whispered, only to have Simon approach from the other side, shaking his head.

"Girls, go home. We'll see you there. There's nothing you can do for anyone here. Are we clear?" By Devon's tone, his inner authoritarian had taken control.

Dani and I looked at each other and shrugged. I reached up on my toes and gave Devon a quick kiss. After I grabbed Dani by the arm, we headed down Main Street toward home. Once we were out of hearing distance, I leaned close to her.

"As soon as we get home, we'll check the camera's uploads."

"You have pictures?" Dani looked at me, then smiled. "Of course you do, being the official town photographer."

"Yes, but I don't just have pictures. I have video."

I had set up a tripod a few feet from the right stage entrance, using a wide-angle lens, and primed the camera to capture video and stills of the moment Hope was to take off my mom's blindfold. I'd also set up a second camera on the catwalk above the rear of the stage. I was sure I'd caught whatever had happened behind the curtain.

Dani nodded approvingly. "Clever." She suddenly stopped as we approached my house. "Did you hear that?" she whispered.

"Hear what?" I asked just as quietly. I stopped breathing for a moment and listened. "I don't hear anything. What did you hear?"

"Like a twig or a branch breaking. It came from your front yard."

We stood on the sidewalk and watched my front yard for signs of movement. After a few moments of nothingness, I shrugged. "The noise was probably just Billy or Skye."

Devon's and my pygmy goats might be having a nighttime romp, though to do so was rare.

"We can check on them, but not dressed like this, I'm afraid. We're liable to step in something." I looked down for emphasis. I wore my new favorite emerald green dress and heels. Not my usual attire. I'd dressed to impress with my long auburn curls worn loose. Dani's coral cocktail dress worked in perfect harmony with her golden Caribbean skin tone and wavy sun-kissed hair. Also in heels, she looked at the muddy yard and grinned.

"Point taken, let's go inside."

Mystic Manor, an old, gothic-style house where occasion-ally strange things happened, was Devon's and my home. A gift from the ladies last year, Devon and I had spent months renovating it, and during those renovations, we'd witnessed several hauntings, like the Native American woman who had ironically appeared in the middle of a séance the ladies had held to find out what could be causing the hauntings at Mystic Manor and other happenings that were going on in their lives at the time.

Morgan and her boyfriend Hunter had eventually laid claim to the hauntings, stating they were filming a paranormal movie. I still didn't believe they'd faked everything that had happened, and right about then, the house had an eerie aura surrounding it, though that could be because our streetlamp was out—which was odd because Luckland's council had recently fitted LED bulbs to all the streetlamps.

I shivered, though it wasn't the house's aura that caused my skin to tighten and the hairs on the back of my neck to stand on end. Something didn't feel right. I turned and looked out onto the darkened street, which was when another snap cracked through the whisper-quiet of the late spring air.

Dani and I whipped around, then strode purposefully up the walkway to the house, where I quickly used the electronic opener on my phone Devon had installed. As soon as we got inside, I flipped on the lights to the foyer, shut the door, locked it, then leaned against it for good measure.

I turned to Dani. "Is it me, or does something feel off to you?"

"Yeah. I just texted Simon. He's on his way."

"Good idea." I wasn't surprised she'd instinctively thought of Simon to come and check outside, though if I questioned Dani about the relationship building between them for over a year, she'd deny anything was going on. They were thirty going on thirteen when it came to acknowledging they had the hots for each other, but I found it funny they'd both decided to come to Luckland for a vacation at the same time—and stay with Devon and me.

I pulled off my shoes, then wiggled my toes. Dani did the same before she pulled me by the arm and headed to the kitchen. "We can check on the goats later. Let's see that video, Pippa. Come on."

Of the same mind, I grabbed my laptop from its perch on the counter, sat at the table, then fired it up while she nabbed a couple of hard ciders from the fridge.

I began to scroll through the video a few frames at a time until a shadow caught my eye. I slowed the video and studied it.

"Lois Thorpe! Holy bat burgers, Dani. Look at this."

"Lois? Town gossip and resident busybody Lois? What about her?"

"She's the reason Matilda screamed."

CHAPTER TWO

"Was it natural causes?" I asked as soon as Devon came in, followed by Simon.

"Was what natural causes?" Devon frowned. "What do you know, and who told you?" He stood tall, legs apart, hands on his hips. He'd dressed for a night on the town in a pair of well-worn jeans with a button-down white cotton shirt, sleeves pushed up, looking hot as hell—and now annoyed as hell. His aquamarine eyes flared as he blew a lock of beautiful chestnut brown hair off his forehead.

"Before you get yourself riled up, come see what I have." I beckoned him by crooking my finger and smiling. Devon strode over and stood behind me.

"There, see it?" I froze the image at the moment when Lois collapsed. "That, Kemosabe, is how I know things."

"Humph," he muttered as he grabbed a chair and sat. Simon headed to the fridge, grabbed a beer for each of them, and returned to the table before grabbing the remaining chair. The thing about Devon and Simon was that they were big guys. Well over six feet tall, broad, and, as I liked to say, handsome devils. Simon was exotic, with his creole caramel complexion and movie star good looks. Devon was more Hollywood-style cowboy cop. Together, the two were an explosive combination.

"So, was it?" I asked.

"Was it what?"

"Was it natural, or do we have a killer on the loose in Luckland?"

"Pretty sure Lois died of natural causes. No signs of foul play. So, you can rein in that imagination of yours," Simon said.

"Lois didn't seem sick to me at the town picnic last week," Dani said. She drained her cider and pushed her chair back. I figured she was headed to get another, but Simon quickly stood.

"I'll get it. Stay," he said.

Dani seemed about to protest, but she relented, a tiny crease marring her brow. I glanced from Dani to Simon and back again. One day they'd get their act together, and I couldn't wait for that day.

"People die suddenly all the time, Dani," Simon said as he returned to the table.

"This is Luckland, Simon. Nothing is ever as it seems," I said as a reminder of the odd things that had happened in town over the past year. "I hope you at least order an autopsy."

"Well, that will depend on the coroner. They'll order one if Lois didn't suffer any medical issues or hadn't seen a doctor recently. If they order one, her sister Louise *could* object, but I'm sure she'd want to find out what happened. We'll be meeting with the coroner and Louise in the morning." Devon looked thoughtful for a moment. "Dani's right, you know. Last week Louise and Lois did the potato sack race. Lois was in fine form. For an older lady."

"Where's the body now?" I asked.

"The medical examiner took Lois to his office." Devon slid

his hand to the back of my neck and tapped his fingers—he was thinking of something.

I was busily thinking of more questions to ask when phones started buzzing. I looked at mine and frowned. "Babs says to hightail it over to the café."

Devon held up his phone. "My mom basically said the same thing."

"When you say basically, you mean what precisely?" I asked.

"Her text said 'Café, now, bring everyone.'"

I looked at Dani. "Mama's says *ven al cafe y mueve tu tresero.*'"

I chuckled. "Translation, please?"

"Well, let's see. Literally, it means 'Come to the café and shake your butt.'" Dani grinned.

Simon laughed. "Gotta love Mama Rosa. I think she meant move your ass, am I right?"

"Either that or it's pole dancing night at the Blue Sky," Dani remarked.

"On that note, shall we?" Devon stood and held out a hand, color highlighting his cheeks. I loved it when he blushed. When we were kids, he always poked and teased me, making me blush —which wasn't hard with me being a freckled-faced redhead. As adults, seeing him blush was karmic.

We headed to the front door, where Dani and I slipped on our shoes, groaning a little at the discomfort. As Devon opened the front door to leave, I stopped short and pulled on his hand.

"The light, you fixed it?"

"Fixed it? No, haven't touched it."

"It was off when we came home."

"And we heard noises too," Dani said, backing me up.

"I'll take a look," Simon said quietly as he slipped by us and headed down the steps to the walkway. He paused every so often, looking about and listening. When he got to the lamp, he lifted the glass housing, then unscrewed the bulb. The sidewalk around him went dark. About a minute later, the light came on again.

"Seems to be fine," he called out. "Let's go before your mothers send the rescue squad."

Main Street in Luckland wasn't all that big, about six blocks long and lined with historic frontier-style buildings—charming for tourists and convenient for those who resided there. Devon and I lived just past the east end of Main Street, while the café sat at the west end. Nobody had technically said it was an emergency, so we walked, though my pinched toes signaled a ride would have been nicer.

I grabbed Devon's hand, still feeling as if something was off. Last year, I'd received a threatening postcard, and soon after, I had the strange sensation of being watched. I felt that sensation again now. Devon didn't seem concerned, nor did Simon. Dani, however, kept glancing over at me. She felt it too.

Entering the bright and airy café, I focused on the posse who all sat at one of the large, counter-height tables Hope and her wife Marcy had recently installed. It was all the rage, apparently. Hope and Marcy owned the café, which they'd moved from their old location to what was once the bakery, attached to the Inn, which they'd also purchased.

They were seated at the new table with my mom, Kate, Dani's mother, Rosa, Devon's mother, Matilda, and Prudence. Babs leaned against the doorway to the kitchen, looking a bit pale. Actually, she looked frightened. My dad had hunkered down in the back with the other spouses, Tom, Trey, and Martin —otherwise now known collectively as the *boys*. That explained why Devon and Simon beelined for the back, leaving Dani and me to face the posse.

"What's this?" I pointed to the board lying in the middle of their table. Each of the women had markers, and they were all scribbling things and marking arrows everywhere. Each of them also had a frosted glass in front of them, with two pitchers of margaritas at the ready.

"We're trying to figure out what happened to dearly departed Loish," Prudence announced.

"You're all three sheets to the wind, aren't you?" I asked, just noticing the additional empty pitchers in the center of the table. I sighed, looked around the table, and raised an eyebrow. "None of you liked Lois."

"Well, shush your mouth, young lady. It's wrong to speak ill of the dead."

Just when I thought the night couldn't get any stranger, I turned toward the voice coming from the front entrance and watched Hilda Feingold, Marcy's aunt, breeze in. Now the nightmare was complete. The nearly ninety-one-year-old author of cozy mysteries grabbed the last remaining chair, then reached over to grab a marker from the Styrofoam cup they'd placed in the middle. After pulling the cap off the marker with her teeth, she leaned in and drew an arrow from what I thought was supposed to be a body but resembled more of a stick figure, and the back of what appeared to be the stage. I had to tilt my head sideways a few times to figure it out.

"Lois was here. Whoever did it came in from here." Hilda waved her arm about to illustrate her point.

"Whoever did what?" I asked. I must have been a little slow on the uptake because it took me a few seconds to realize what she was talking about. When I had, I almost groaned aloud. Trust the posse to automatically assume someone murdered Lois.

"Well, I think that frozen heart of hers just gave out." Hope sighed and swayed on her stool.

Spinning stools were a very bad idea. Concerned the women

really needed to sit lower to the ground, in chairs, I glanced around the café. However, every seat was taken.

"I'm going to need all your car keys," I said firmly, holding out my hand.

"We came afoot," Matilda said.

"Afoot?" I tried to stop myself from rolling my eyes as Dani bit back a grin.

"Maybe Louise did it," my mother whispered. "You know, I heard those two sisters were jealous of each other. Scratched each other's eyes out once."

Babs came over and glanced down at the board before she nervously scanned the regular customers. "From where I was sitting, I saw someone go out the back," she said quietly.

My camera hadn't caught anyone leaving the back of the theater, and I frowned. "Could have been anyone, Babs."

Hilda shook her head. "I bet it was the killer."

www.scarsdalepublishing.com

THE LUCKLAND MYSTERY SERIES

Grande Dames and a Vegas Heist
Aliens and the Dearly Departed
Mislaid Love and Found Bodies
Stolen Recipes and a Dead Chef
Vengeful Spirits and a Lost Gold Mine

More to come!

www.ingramcontent.com/pod-product-compliance
Lightning Source LLC
Chambersburg PA
CBHW061440210726
48287CB00007B/2293